THE
END
OF THE
SIDEWALK

THE
END
OF THE
SIDEWALK

Nancy Schutt McCorkle

Copyright © 2025 by Nancy Schutt McCorkle

All rights reserved.
This book, or parts thereof, may not be
reproduced in any form without permission.

Paperback ISBN: 978-1-63337-988-6
E-Book ISBN: 978-1-63337-989-3

Printed in the United States of America
1 3 5 7 9 10 8 6 4 2

In memory of my Mom, Jane Page Menefee Schutt,
and my Dad, Wallis Isham Schutt, who both inspired this story.

For my dandy man, Ken, and my children, John, Patricia,
and Page, who believed in me and encouraged me to persevere,
and for Jane Monachelli, who is part of the story.

CHAPTER 1

AUGUST 26, 1961

I couldn't wait to see *The Parent Trap*. I felt like everyone had seen it before me. It was the perfect thing for my twelfth birthday, and my cousin Sarah Jane and I were going to see it together. That was perfect too. She wasn't just my cousin but my best friend. Even though she was nine months older, today we would be the same age.

Aunt Liz had barely stopped the car before we ran out to get our tickets. I knew the movie would remind us of Girl Scout Camp because it was about twins at a camp. Sarah Jane and I hooked pinkies, our secret signal that we were best friends forever, and we both laughed. She looked pretty in her navy pleated skirt and blue blouse. Her blue eyes matched her outfit. I wore my favorite denim jumper with a white blouse and my cowboy boots.

"Hey, look," someone yelled.

We turned around to see a caravan of five police cars passing by. There were no flashing lights, but they were driving fast.

"What's going on?" I asked the person in front of us.

"It's those crazy Freedom Riders coming on the bus," he said.

The words *Freedom Riders* stirred something inside me. I wanted to see them. I knew about them from the news and from hearing Mom and Dad talk about them. I grabbed Sarah Jane's

THE END OF THE SIDEWALK

hand, pulled her out of line, then ran down the sidewalk toward the police cars, dragging her along.

"Wait, where are we going?" she yelled as she jerked my arm.

"I want to check out the Freedom Riders. Mom might be there. She said she had a meeting downtown."

"What? Are you crazy? Who are the Freedom Riders? I don't want to miss the movie." She stopped me dead still, planting her feet solidly on the ground.

"Listen, don't you know? The Freedom Riders are Negro people and white people riding the bus together and trying to integrate the bus station. Mom's been concerned about them. She might be there to support them."

"I'll go if you promise we won't stay long," she said.

"I promise, but we need to hurry." I grabbed her hand, and we dodged in and out of people walking down the wide sidewalk. We ran two blocks past office buildings and the Emporium department store. The mannequins, in their shirtwaist dresses and pillbox hats, stared out at us from the window. When we reached the bus station, big red capital letters spelled *TRAILWAYS* on the front of the building. Police cars lined the drive.

But there wasn't a big crowd like I had expected. Sarah Jane and I eased in behind the group of white protesters standing in front of the station. I didn't see any children, just some men and women. Some were holding signs. One said *Go Home, Yankees*. Another said *Separate but Equal*. We moved toward the middle of the group, trying to blend in, and then peeked around the people in front of us in time to see the bus pulling into the depot with the policemen standing there waiting for it. What was going to happen?

"Your mom's not here," Sarah Jane said. "I don't see her anywhere. Let's go. You promised, Trudy." She grabbed my arm, and her dark curls bounced as she glared at me. "I'm serious. Let's go back to the theater. This is no way to spend your birthday."

I heard the bus's brakes screech as it pulled in. I jumped back, bumping into Sara Jane.

"Watch out! You're stepping on my toe." She pulled on my arm.

"Sorry. Don't stand so close. Will you give me a little room? We'll leave in just a minute."

My legs trembled, yet I was excited to see a real Freedom Rider. I knew that they must be scared. I knew I was. I was shaking even though it was hot as the dickens.

The driver stepped off the bus, opened a hatch, and unloaded suitcases onto the walkway. Several white people got off, then some Black people got off too. One guy wore a Harvard T-shirt, another wore an Ohio State shirt.

"It's the Freedom Riders," I said. Sarah Jane pulled me back again as I tried to get a good look. My heart pounded like a metronome on fast speed.

"Come on, let's go," Sarah Jane said. "I'm scared. What's going to happen to them?" She tugged on my shirt. "Somebody's going to see us. My mom will be furious if she finds out I was here."

"Quit holding me. I'm not going out there. The police are going to arrest them and take them to jail for disturbing the peace."

"What?" Sarah Jane whispered.

"I'll tell you later."

A white girl and a Black girl walked right to the doors of the bus depot's waiting rooms. One door had a sign that said *WHITE* and the other door was marked *COLORED*. A policeman stopped one of the Colored guys as he walked through the door to the white waiting room and said something to him. I couldn't hear what he said, but then he took the guy's arm and pushed him to the police van out front. The policeman made him get into the van. People called it a paddy wagon. I didn't know why.

"You better come on, I've seen enough," Sarah Jane whispered. A part of me thought we should leave, but I also wanted to see what happened.

Several policemen surrounded the group, pushing them over to the paddy wagon. The Freedom Riders bumped into each other. A white girl stumbled and fell.

Two policemen moved toward her, then one of them took her arm, pulled her up, and yelled in her face, "Yankee woman, you need to . . ." I strained to hear the rest, but his voice was muffled. She didn't say anything but looked straight ahead and got into the van.

Sarah Jane yanked on me. "I'm leaving." She started backing up from the group.

My stomach tightened. I thought my mom might have been here, but I was glad she wasn't because she would have walked right out there and helped the girl up. Then she might have been arrested with the Freedom Riders.

A hum came from inside the paddy wagon. It got louder and louder as the people inside it belted out the song "We Shall Overcome."

A policeman slammed the door and stomped around to the front. "Shut up!" he shouted, but we could still hear them singing like a choir.

One policeman started walking toward us. I turned to see where Sarah Jane was, and I ran to catch up with her.

The policeman yelled, "Hey, you two come here right now." We did as we were told, and he said, "What are you girls doing down here? Don't you know it's dangerous? You have no business being here."

"We're . . . we're going to the movies," Sarah Jane stammered.

"No, you're not. I'm taking you home. What's your name, and where do you live?"

"Sarah Jane Hartman, 1053 Claiborne Avenue." She gave me the meanest look. Then I said, "Uh . . . uh . . . Gertrude Scuffer, uh . . . 955 Pecan Boulevard." He dropped his pencil. I could hardly breathe. Any brave thoughts I had flew right out of my head like a bird flying in the sky.

"Spell your last name," he said as he picked up the pencil and wrote.

"*S-c-u-f-f-e-r*," I replied, trying to keep my voice steady.

"Do your parents know that you're down here?"

I shook my head.

"You should have gone to the movies." He shook his head. "This is no place for two girls. We don't want any trouble here like the bus burning they had in Alabama. Scuffer. Yes, that name rings a bell. Your mom's the one on that commission riling up the Coloreds."

I wanted to say my mom was helping, but when I opened my mouth, nothing came out.

Sarah Jane twisted one of her curls. A tear slid down her face, and her lips quivered. She said to me in a loud whisper, "Why did you make me do this? You knew I didn't want to."

"I'm sorry," I whispered back. I wanted to comfort her, but I didn't know what else to say. In the police car, a cage window separated us from the front seat. I knew Dad would be mad if he saw a police car pull up in front of our house with me in it. Sarah Jane stared out the side window the whole time. She wouldn't even look at me.

The policeman took her home first. As she got out of the car, she turned to me, stuck out her tongue, and then did our secret signal. After she hooked her pinkies together, she then broke them apart and shook her hands like she was rid of me. She stuck out her tongue again, and ran into her house without looking back.

Aunt Liz came to the door and stood with her arms crossed, talking to the policeman. Then she turned, went into the house, and shut the door behind her. I was left alone like a prisoner.

I always thought my street was one of the prettiest in Jackson, Mississippi. It was the only street in West Jackson that had islands dividing the street with pecan trees and azalea bushes inside those islands. It was beautiful in the spring. Today when the policeman turned onto Pecan Boulevard, I wished I was on any street but mine. Our house was eight houses from the corner. Big wide sidewalks were on either side of the street, and I loved skating up and down the middle of the street. I knew now I should have stayed at the movie, but it was too late for thinking about that. The policeman pulled into our driveway. Mom's car was gone.

I sat as still as a statue. When the policeman opened the door and told me to get out of the police car, I said a little prayer in my head. I really wanted to scream that I was sorry and then take off running.

Dad frowned when he opened the door. I couldn't even look at him. I tried not to, but I burst into tears.

"Are you Gertrude Scuffer's father?" the policeman said. "Is your wife the one on that commission stirring up the Colored people? I think your daughter's trying to follow in her footsteps. You better get things under control."

"Yes, I'm Warren Scuffer. Sir, no disrespect, but you need to watch what you say. Now, what happened?"

"Young lady, tell your dad where I found you," the policeman said.

A shiver ran down my back as the words came out. "Uh . . . we . . . went to see the Freedom Riders."

"Get in the house," Dad said with such a firm tone that the policeman looked startled.

"Yes, sir," I mumbled as I scooted by him. Who'd have ever thought I'd end up in a police car on my birthday? Heck, I'd messed up my birthday for sure.

Plopping down on my bed, I stared at the rain stain on the ceiling. My head hurt, and it wouldn't stop. I grabbed my quilt, pulled it over my head, and prayed I would disappear. My heart was racing like I'd been running for miles. I tried to take deep breaths. Was this what a heart attack felt like?

CHAPTER 2

I PEEKED out from under the quilt and grabbed my favorite book, *Donna and Thunder*. I had read it four times and longed to be like Donna. She had a horse and could ride any time she wanted. She also could talk her way out of trouble almost every time. I was scared to say anything when I was in trouble.

I wanted a horse so bad I would do anything to help. I could babysit, rake yards when the leaves fell, and pick up pecans in other people's yards. Even if I had a slight chance to get a horse before, I knew what happened today wouldn't help at all. I hoped Mom and Dad would understand why I went to see the Freedom Riders, but I had a queasy feeling that it wasn't going to be like that at all.

"Gertrude Randolph, come here," Mom said after she got home. Whenever she used my middle name, I knew she meant business. Throwing back my quilt and swallowing hard, I eased out my door to meet my fate.

"Young lady, what happened today will be addressed after supper. Do you understand?" Mom said with a scowl on her face. "Liz and your cousins will be here shortly."

"Yes, ma'am." Struggling to stand still, I stared at my boots. If I'd had a horse in the backyard, I would've run out and jumped on its back and taken off. Instead, I turned and ran to the bathroom. Sitting on the edge of the tub, I buried my face in a washcloth and cried like a baby. After a few minutes, I splashed some cold water on my eyes, then cupped my hands and took a few gulps of water. How would I make it through supper? I had to get control of myself.

A knock sounded at the door. "Hurry up. I need to wash my hands," my brother Joseph said.

"Okay, okay. I'm almost done." I didn't want him to know I'd been crying. Most of the time he was easy to get along with, but eight-year-olds wouldn't understand this. After I opened the door, I pushed by him as fast as I could.

"Don't say anything about today," I whispered as I sat down at the table next to Sarah Jane. She frowned at me. Although we'd been cousins and best friends our whole life, she didn't act like it now. Her brother Frank talked to Joseph as they sat across from us. Frank didn't seem to know what happened.

"Happy Birthday, Trudy," Frank said smiling at me.

"Thanks." Oh, how I wanted it to be happy, but I knew better.

The kitchen door swung open as Mom and Aunt Liz brought in the fried chicken, mashed potatoes, green beans, and homemade biscuits. They put it all on the table. It was my favorite meal, but tonight I didn't feel like eating. Even the sight of good food couldn't stir my appetite.

Aunt Liz didn't even look at me. Though the smell of hot biscuits normally made my mouth water, tonight the looming talk after supper made my mouth dry. I forced myself to eat, keeping my eye on those presents lined up on the buffet. I even felt guilty about the presents being for me when I was certain everyone was mad at me. I stared at the ladies in long dresses under ivy trellises that were on the wallpaper that covered the dining room and hall.

I once counted one hundred and thirty-three ladies in all. Now I wondered what they did when they were in trouble, and I wanted to fade into the wallpaper with them to avoid that talk that I knew was going to happen. Unlike other suppers, no one talked during the entire meal, except for Frank and Joseph chatting with each other.

Mom and I both flinched when the phone rang, ending the uncomfortable silence. Dad threw his napkin down, yanked the phone out of its cradle, and almost tripped over the cord.

"Hello? Hello?"

Dad slammed the phone down and everybody froze. He said, "I'm sick and tired of these phone calls every night. We can't even finish a meal without interruption. When's it going to stop?"

"I'll answer it next time it rings," Mom said. Ever since Mom got on the civil rights commission, someone called every night.

"No, you won't," Dad said.

Aunt Liz got up from the table and took her plate into the kitchen with food still on it. Sarah Jane and Mom got up and followed her. I heard Mom say, "Don't leave yet."

I also started to get up, but Dad pushed back his chair, blocking the way.

"Sit down, Trudy," he said as Mom came into the room singing the "Happy Birthday" song. I half-smiled at everyone, trying to act like nothing was wrong. She set in front of me a butterscotch pie that Jetta Mae had made, my absolute favorite. Jetta Mae had worked for us as long as my memory. She knew what I would like. Mom couldn't put candles in the fluffy meringue, so she set one tall burning candle in a silver candle holder by the pie. Aunt Liz wiped her eyes with a tissue. Even though they sang, it didn't feel like a celebration. Dad looked serious instead of showing his usual big smile. Joseph and Frank were the only ones having a good time.

The tips of the white meringue shone in the light. The golden-brown crust stuck up around the edges of the plate. When I blew out the candle, I wished that Mom and Dad wouldn't be upset. Holy Moley, why did I waste my wish? I could see trouble brewing by the looks on their faces. I should have wished for a horse.

Mom cut slices and passed them out. I stuck my fork in the creamy butterscotch custard and savored that first bite. Yum, the meringue melted in my mouth. I forgot for a minute the mood affecting my birthday. If only I hadn't gone to the bus station, everything would be different.

Mom brought the presents to the table. The first gift I opened was from Aunt Liz and Sarah Jane, the book *Misty of Chincoteague*. Aunt Liz knew how I liked books about horses.

"Thank you, thank you. I can't wait to read it," I said. I took a deep breath as Aunt Liz gave me a slight smile, but Sarah Jane's cold stare rattled me. Mom gave me a new pair of shorts and a shirt. Then Dad pulled out a box from under the table and handed it to me. In it was a beautiful brown porcelain horse. I opened the card that was with it.

> *I know you want a real horse. But the feed bill is too high.*
> *So this little glass horse is all I can supply.*
>
> *Love, Dad*

"Thanks, Dad. I love it." I didn't want to seem ungrateful, but looking at that horse every day was going to make me want a real one even more.

"Thanks for my present," I said as Sarah Jane walked to the living room without waiting for me. I followed and sat on the loveseat beside her. "We've always stuck together. You're really mad at me, aren't you?"

She crossed her arms and said, "You got me in big trouble. Mom's furious."

"I'm sorry, but there's nothing I can do about it now. Maybe when I explain, she won't be so mad. Please, let's stick together."

Mom, Dad, and Aunt Liz came in and sat down. Why couldn't they give me a little break since it was my birthday? I took three deep breaths, but it didn't help.

"Okay, Gertrude, now's your chance to tell us exactly what happened today," Dad said.

"We went . . . no, I went . . . I wanted to see the brave people on the bus, and I thought Mom might be there too. I didn't think it would hurt anything. When the Freedom Riders got off the bus, we saw them get arrested. We got scared and were leaving when the policeman stopped us."

Sarah Jane twisted her hair and looked down. I saw her lip trembling.

"Don't ever do anything like that again," Dad said. "Do I make myself clear?"

"Yes, sir."

"I told you I had a meeting," Mom said. "The authorities warned people to stay away from the bus station. They didn't want trouble here like they had in Alabama. Did you girls think about that?"

"No, ma'am," I said. "The policeman told us that too. He also said you were on the commission to rile up the Coloreds."

"The commission is a committee to hear the wrongs that the Negroes have endured and to report them to Washington DC. The Freedom Riders are working for equal rights in transportation. I'm not trying to rile up anyone. I'm trying to help."

Aunt Liz said, "I've heard enough. Come on, we're leaving. I won't have my children involved in this."

"Wait, Liz," Mom said. "Let's talk, please."

"You can be on your commission and do what you like, but I'll have no part in it. You can't change laws that have been in place for ages." She went and got Frank and left in a huff. Sarah Jane didn't even look back at me as they hurried out the door.

Mom and Dad were quiet for a minute, then Dad said, "You're on restriction this week for going without permission. That means no phone calls or going to play with friends. Jetta Mae can use your help around the house."

I nodded in agreement. What else could I do?

"Young lady, go get your pajamas on. It's early to bed for you tonight."

I left in a rush to my bedroom, slammed my door in frustration, and fell on my bed. My door handle turned, and the door flew open.

"We don't slam doors around here," Dad said. "I'll not have you being disrespectful." Dad meant business. I could tell.

"I'm sorry." I buried my head in my pillow.

"Good night," he said and closed my door.

I drenched my pillowcase with tears. I wished Mom would come in, stroke my head, and tell me everything was going to be all right. I didn't even want to be twelve. I was starting junior high school in two weeks, and I double-dog dreaded it. I pulled out my diary from under my pillow but didn't feel like writing much, so I wrote a short poem.

Promise.
Today is gone with its tear of sorrow.
Now go to sleep and dream of tomorrow.

CHAPTER 3

OUR DOG Skipper's barking woke me up, and the first thought that popped into my head was my restriction. I couldn't call Sarah Jane and try to make up. What would I do if I couldn't straighten things out with her before school started? I wanted her to show me the ropes. She'd been at Hardy Junior High School for a whole year, so I wouldn't be nervous if I walked in with her on my first day. In two weeks, school started on September 5th. Yikes!

I realized that I'd better do some planning. I wanted to be popular, but I was still a Girl Scout. Most people my age thought that was for little kids. I also needed to figure out a way to have a horse, but Dad had put a damper on that when he gave me the porcelain horse last night.

Trying out my new shorts and shirt from Mom, they fit me perfectly. I put on my cowboy boots. There were my favorite shoes because I thought they hid my size ten feet. Even though Sarah Jane was taller, she only wore size eight. Finally dressed, I grabbed *Misty of Chincoteague* and started down the hallway. I heard Mom and Dad talking.

"I don't think bringing Colored women in our house is a good idea right now," Dad said.

"I don't see why not," Mom said. "It's our house. I don't want to disappoint these ladies. Father Samuel wouldn't let us meet at

THE END OF THE SIDEWALK

St. Columb's. We need to pray for the Freedom Riders and all the unrest going on. I need your support. You said you would help me."

"How many women are we talking about?"

"Probably about a dozen. A couple of Freedom Riders are coming to talk to us. Clarie Harvey, the president of Womanpower Unlimited, is coming too."

"Well, I need to be in Picayune all day, and I won't be back until late tonight. I don't like this going on when I'm not here. Can't you do it a different night?"

"I'd have to call everyone. Please let me do it this one time. It'll be fine."

"I guess you can do it, but make sure the meeting doesn't run too late."

"Oh, I will. Thanks, Honey."

Dad headed out the front door. I took a deep breath before going into the kitchen.

"Ouch." My knee had bumped the chrome pedestal of our yellow Formica breakfast table as I'd tried to slip my legs under it. The little brown lines which formed the design on the yellow background reminded me of tic-tac-toe lines. The table always looked shiny and was easy to clean.

Mom set a plate of French toast in front of me. It made me think of a giraffe's skin with its brown and yellow shapes. Joseph straggled in with his blond hair sticking up in all directions. He sat down and started gobbling his breakfast down in a hurry.

"You two, Jetta Mae will be here any minute," Mom said. "I'm going downtown, and your dad went to Picayune. I'm having a meeting here tonight. You can help get things ready."

"What kind of meeting?" Joseph asked.

"Some ladies from St. Mark's, the Black Episcopal church."

I heard a noise, and Jetta Mae walked in from the living room. She had just started using the front door after all the years of using the back door. Mom insisted we were going to make some changes, and Jetta Mae had agreed to change her ways.

"I'm having a meeting here tonight," Mom said to Jetta Mae. "Could you set up the living room for about twelve people? And will you be joining us?"

"Oh, I don't know. I'd like to, but my mother's been feeling poorly, and I think I'd better go on home at my regular time." Jetta Mae's thick black hair was piled in rolls on the top of her head. She put on a white starched apron over her green dress. Her plump size made her seem bigger than Mom, but she was about the same height.

"Gertrude will help you with everything," Mom said.

"Yes, indeedy," I said. I loved talking to Jetta Mae and helping her. I could tell her anything.

"Please, please stay," I begged after Mom left. If Jetta Mae stayed, I would feel better about the meeting. She was the only Black person I really knew.

"We'll see. I would like to meet those ladies and pray with them," she said. I went over and hugged her.

"Thanks for the yummy pie," I said. "We ate every bit of it. Everything was delicious. You're the best. I got some nice presents but no real horse. Dad gave me a little one. Wait. I'll show it to you." I ran to my room, picked up the horse off my dresser, and brought it back to show her.

"Now that's a mighty pretty thing," she said.

Then I whispered in her ear, "I'm on restriction."

"Whatever for?" she asked. I told her what happened, then she said, "Yes ma'am, you need to stay away from the bus station."

"I wanted to see what was going on, but Mom and Dad said it was dangerous. They said that, after the bus burning in Alabama, our policemen wanted to make sure nothing like that happened here."

"It's a shame we all can't get along." Jetta Mae shook her head as she set up her ironing board. "Some white people think they're better than we are and make us sit in the back of the bus. You know about Rosa Parks, don't you?"

"No, is she a friend of yours?"

"No, no. She lives in Montgomery, Alabama. She refused to give up her seat at the front of the bus to a white man, and they arrested her. Martin Luther King Jr. came, got everyone organized, then all the Negroes decided to stop riding the buses. None rode the buses for a year, and the officials changed the law so Negroes could sit anywhere on the bus. That doesn't apply here, though."

"Well, it should. I'm glad you told me about her and Martin Luther King Jr." I loved talking to Jetta Mae. She listened to me, and she always told me something important. "Have you ever heard of the White Citizens Council?" I asked.

Jetta Mae nodded and said, "They want everything separate between Black people and white people. They don't want any mixing, no they don't." Jetta Mae shook her head. "Do you know about the NAACP?"

"No, what's that?"

"It's the National Association for the Advancement of Colored People. Right now, we're working to get people registered to vote. The White Citizen's Council doesn't like that either.

They don't want my people voting. They think we're not as smart as they are."

"Are you registered to vote?" I asked her. I wanted to know what was so important about it.

"Yes, ma'am. I got to vote for President Kennedy. Now I'm working a couple of hours a week to help others register."

"Why is registering such a big deal?"

"Many white people don't want us to vote. They don't think we're qualified, and set different rules for us. Some of my people don't know how to read because they had to work instead of going to school, so some white folks think they shouldn't be allowed to vote. Some don't even want them around at all. That bus burning in Alabama . . . *tsk, tsk*. Don't know why people act so vicious." She looked at me and smiled. "Say, are you wearing a new outfit? My, my, you are growing up tall and pretty."

Jetta Mae always found something nice to say, but I didn't think I was pretty. My knock knees and long skinny legs stuck out from my shorts like stakes for tomato plants.

"Would you be a Freedom Rider?" I asked her.

"No, I'm not cut out for that sort of thing, but I do want to help my people get treated right. I like working behind the scenes."

"I wouldn't want to be one, either, because I wouldn't want to go to jail. I want you to be treated right too. Did you know that Sarah Jane got mad at me because we got in trouble? Now we won't be able to talk for a week. I'm afraid she won't be my best friend anymore."

"I wouldn't worry too much. She'll be back over here before you know it. Now go in there and practice your piano."

THE END OF THE SIDEWALK

"Ugh." I hated the piano because I couldn't keep the rhythm without hitting the wrong notes. On the other hand, Sarah Jane played by ear. Her fingers ran up and down the keys without missing a note. Mom always bragged about her. After five years, I should have made it to Book Five, but I was still in Book Two. Sarah Jane was already in Book Five.

"Go do your best," Jetta Mae said. Don't think so hard about it, and it might come easier."

I sat down at the piano and stared at the black and white keys. A hard song used both colors of keys to make beautiful music. Why couldn't Black people and white people do the same? That's what Mom wanted. What did I want? I wanted everybody to get along with each other, especially Mom, Dad, and Aunt Liz. I didn't understand why it had to be such a big deal between everyone.

I struggled through my practice, and after fifteen minutes I went back into the kitchen with Jetta Mae.

"Take your dad's shirts, please," she said.

When I hung the white starched shirts in Mom and Dad's closet, I stepped into Mom's little office off their bedroom and some letters that were open on Mom's desk caught my eye. Unable to resist, I picked one up and started reading.

> *Dear June,*
>
> *I admire your courageous decision. Your leadership will be invaluable, and there is hope for change with people like you. You are in my thoughts and prayers. Hold your head high.*
>
> *Your friend, Lois*

Nancy Schutt McCorkle

I liked what Mom's friend said even though I didn't know her. Maybe I needed to try and hold my head high. I picked up another one with the heading "From the Office of the Mayor." I fumbled as I tried to read it, hoping Jetta Mae wouldn't come around the corner. I probably shouldn't have been reading it, but I wanted to know what was going on so I could help our family get back together instead of staying in the mess we were in right now.

Dear Mrs. Scuffer,

Why do you think anyone wants to listen to your stupid remarks? Don't you know that the commission is against what everyone in Mississippi wants? I am ashamed of you and your decision. I am sure your children will never have cause to be proud that you served in such a subversive group. The commission will never do the South any good and neither can you. You're not a native Mississippian, so how do you think you can represent our state? You can't.

Sickened by you,
W. S. Comer, Mayor of Itta Bena

My face heated up, and my hands shook. I laid the letter back down. How could that man say that I wouldn't be proud of my mom and that he was sickened by her? I had a good mind to write him back and give him my opinion. I wasn't sure what subversive meant, but it didn't sound complimentary.

Back in the kitchen, I pushed the chair hard against the floor.

"What's got into you?" Jetta Mae asked.

"Nothing. What does subversive mean?"

"It has to do with going against the government, like Rosa Parks did. Where did you hear that word?" She wiped the perspiration from her brow.

"I don't know. I saw it somewhere." I didn't want to tell her about the letter. She'd scold me for snooping.

"Why don't you go look it up in the dictionary?"

In the living room, the bookshelves extended from the ceiling to the floor. I found the dictionary and looked up the word. *Subversive: intended to overthrow or undermine an established government; to ruin or destroy.*

I reported back to Jetta Mae, "It was just like you said. Do you think the commission that Mom is on is subversive?"

"Of course not. My people need to be heard." Jetta Mae started ironing a part she had already ironed. She probably wanted me to stop bugging her.

"I have another question for you about something different," I said. "Do you think I could save enough money to buy a horse? I want one in the worst way."

"Goodness gracious, child. Your questions are all over the place today."

"Well, what do you think?" I asked, crossing my arms and trying to stand like a cowboy.

"Hmm. Where would you keep it? How would you make enough money to feed it if you had one?"

"I don't know. Maybe I could keep it in that pasture up there on Claiborne Avenue. I could walk there every day and ride it."

"I think you could save your money to go ride at Miller Stables, but it would take a lot more money to buy a horse. Talk to your mom about it. She'll understand." Jetta Mae put her hands on her hips.

"She's so busy. I'll try and ask her. Do you have any dreams about things you want?"

"Well, I've dreamed about having my own bakery one day." Jetta Mae looked as if she was picturing it in her mind.

"Wow, that would be great. Everybody would buy your pies and cakes. They're so delicious."

"Well, it's not likely to happen, but maybe someday. Now go set up the chairs in the living room for the meeting, please."

I started to go into the living room when the phone rang. I answered it. They asked to speak to Jetta Mae. She took the phone, then she put the receiver down, wailing, "Oh no! Oh no!" as she covered her face with her hands.

CHAPTER 4

"WHAT'S WRONG? Tell me," I said as Jetta Mae hung up the phone and rushed to get her purse.

"My mother's ill," Jetta Mae said, "and she's taken a turn for the worse. I must leave now. Tell your mom I'll get in touch with her. She should be home in a few minutes" Jetta Mae walked out the front door and hurried away.

It wasn't too long before Mom got home. I ran to her. "Jetta Mae's mom is very sick. She left in a hurry."

"Oh, dear. Her mom's been sick for over a week now. I'll give her a call." Mom dialed the phone. After they talked, Mom said, "They called the doctor, and he'll see her tomorrow."

Joseph, Mom, and I ate supper in the kitchen since Dad wasn't home yet.

"Gertrude, I'll need your help tonight," Mom said. "Joseph, I want you to stay in your room and play while the ladies are here."

I didn't know what I could do to help, but I was curious about what they were going to say and do. I hoped that they wouldn't notice my nervousness. When I scraped my leftovers into Skipper's bowl, I hoped Mom hadn't seen how little I'd eaten.

Ding dong.

Mom wiped her hands, rushed into the living room, and opened the door. Dressed like they were going to church, eight

Negro ladies walked into our living room. I stood in the dining room and arranged the napkins on the table.

"We came in two cars so that there wouldn't be so many parked outside your house," one lady said.

Maybe the neighbors wouldn't even notice, I thought. The doorbell rang again, and in walked a white girl with a single blond braid and a Negro girl with short black hair. Mom called me over.

"Caroline and Justine, this is my daughter Gertrude. She's helping me out tonight."

Caroline grabbed my hand and said, "I'm glad to meet you." Justine squeezed my hand and smiled. Mom said they were real Freedom Riders. I wanted to tell them how brave they were, but Mom was ready to start the meeting. She opened her prayer book and read, "O God, who hast made of one blood all nations of men to dwell on the face of the whole earth and who didst send thy blessed son to preach peace to them that are far off and to them that are nigh, grant that all men everywhere may seek after thee and find thee. Bring all nations into thy fold. Pour out thy spirit upon all flesh and hasten thy kingdom through thy son Jesus Christ our Lord, Amen."

After Mom closed her prayer book, she said, "Thank you all for coming. Tonight, we're fortunate to have two of our young Freedom Riders here to share their experience with us." She leaned over and told me to go fix the plates with cake and to pour the coffee. I frowned because I wanted to hear what they had to say. I tiptoed to the kitchen and hoped I could sneak back in before they finished. In no time, I slipped back into the dining room where I couldn't be seen.

Justine stood up first, straightened her plaid skirt, and said, "Good evening, ladies. I'm Justine Thompson, and I'm a sophomore at Indiana State. When I volunteered to be a Freedom Rider, I wasn't sure what to expect. I knew it was risky because according to some state laws, we're not to use the Whites-only waiting room. But that isn't right according to federal law. A group of us came from my college, but I didn't expect the treatment we received. All the women were put in one big room at Parchman Prison. It was crowded, and there were no beds. We slept on the floor without pillows or blankets. They didn't give us toothbrushes or soap. The guards laughed if we asked for anything."

Caroline stood, her long navy-blue skirt swishing at her ankles. She clasped her hands in front of her. "Justine and I rode the bus down here together. We were arrested for disturbing the peace. We kept saying *Jail, no bail* because we wanted them to know we didn't do anything to disturb the peace. In the prison, the guards brought us beans and rice to eat almost every day. We sang songs all the time. The guards didn't like us singing, so they took the screens off the windows and the mosquitoes started biting us. When we complained, they sprayed DDT in the room. People began coughing and getting sick. The guards didn't even care."

I knew from running behind the DDT truck that the smoke made me cough. I couldn't imagine having it sprayed in a room. I could hardly breathe just thinking about it. Why did the guards have to be so mean?

"We stood together," she said. "They let us go so we could go back to school, but we had to pay a fine. We're proud to stand up for what's right. We shall overcome someday."

One woman stood up and said, "Amen, sister." Then Mom stood up and said, "Ladies, our friend, Mrs. Clarie Harvey, has

THE END OF THE SIDEWALK

started a program called Womanpower Unlimited. She has some ideas of things we can do."

Mrs. Harvey said, "First, we can fix some bags for the women at Parchman, send them toothbrushes, soap, and washcloths. We can help in that way."

Maybe I shouldn't have listened, but now I knew some more hard things that the Freedom Riders were facing. I hurried to serve the cake and coffee and hoped no one had seen me listening.

Then everyone stood, held hands, and started singing "We Shall Overcome," just like the Freedom Riders in the paddy wagon had done. I squeezed in between Caroline and Justine, then looked at Mom. Like always, she had her eyes closed as she sang. I wanted to be brave like Caroline and Justine, and maybe I would be a Freedom Rider someday.

The ladies were getting ready to leave when the sound of sirens blared outside. They got louder and louder. Mom opened the front door and looked out. Red lights flashed outside as a fire truck stopped right in front of our house.

"Someone reported a fire here," one fireman yelled as other firemen started hooking a hose to the fire hydrant by the curb in front of our house. Joseph ran into the living room and out the front door. Yikes! I wanted to go hide in the kitchen.

"Wow, a fire truck," Joseph said. "Why are they here?" Mom grabbed his shirt and pulled him back up the steps.

"Stop!" she yelled. "You're mistaken. There's no fire here. Please, listen."

"Lady, did you call?" A fireman came up the steps and peered in the door. All the ladies sat in the chairs, not saying a word. He looked startled. "What's going on here? Hey, Mark, come here," he said, calling another fireman to the door.

"Well, well, what have we here?" Mark said. "Now aren't they dressed up pretty? Looks like they're having a little tea party," he said in a sarcastic voice.

"We're having a prayer group," Mom said. "No one called from here about a fire. You've made a mistake. Please go now." Mom had spoken in a calm voice with her arms around Joseph. I stayed behind Mom, shivering like a cold wind was blowing.

"You all better be careful going home," Mark said. The other fireman shook his head and muttered to himself as they rolled up the hose. They left without lights and siren, but they let the bells clang so the neighborhood knew something was going on at our house. Aunt Liz probably heard it at her house and would be more upset with Mom.

The ladies sat in stunned silence. Some wrung their hands. Then Mom said, "Let us pray." She started the Lord's Prayer, and everyone joined in with her.

"Mrs. Scuffer," one lady said, "we're sorry. We're leaving right now. We don't want any trouble." They all prepared to leave.

"Someone must have called the fire department on purpose," another woman said.

"We weren't doing anything wrong or hurting anyone," Mom said. "This is my house, and I can invite any guests I choose into my home." Mom tried to end on a positive note, but the arrival of the fire truck and the rude remarks by the firemen had put everyone on edge, including me.

As soon as the women left, I ran to Mom. "Who do you think called the fire department? Who knew about your meeting?"

THE END OF THE SIDEWALK

I stared at her, wide-eyed and scared.

"I don't know. Perhaps someone saw the ladies coming into the house. Some people will do anything to cause a disturbance. Let's get things cleaned up. Don't worry."

"I heard someone talking about the Jim Crow laws. Are they real laws?"

Joseph joined us and started moving the chairs back into the dining room.

Mom said, "They're laws formed by states in the South to make sure the schools and public places stay segregated. They want everything separated between Negroes and Whites, and I think that's wrong. The laws make it hard for Negroes to vote and make them pay a poll tax and pass a test, but those laws don't require the same of white people. It isn't fair."

"Who's Jim Crow?" Joseph asked. I didn't even know he was listening.

"It's just what those laws are called and not a real person," Mom said. "The laws have been around a long time, but that doesn't make them right. Negroes are not treated fairly."

I didn't know what to think. I'd never even been around any Colored people except Jetta Mae. Mom said we should call them Negroes now and be as nice to them as anyone else. I needed to study up on it all and see what I could find out. Then I'd ask Mom more and Jetta Mae could tell me her side of it.

"Mom, can Skipper sleep in my room tonight?" I said. I would feel safer if he was with me.

"I guess so."

Once I got in bed and turned out the light, I heard something. Skipper raised his head.

"Trudy?" Joseph whispered as he opened my bedroom door. "Can I sleep in here tonight?" He climbed up the ladder into the top bunk before I could say anything. I welcomed his company. We were both scared.

"Night, sleep tight, don't let the bedbugs bite," I said, then reached down, petted Skipper, and drifted off to sleep.

CHAPTER 5

NEXT MORNING when Jetta Mae came in the back door, I saw that something was wrong. She looked like she was about to puke. Her hair was uncombed, and her eyes looked weak.

"What on earth is wrong with you?" Mom asked as she rushed over to grab Jetta Mae's arm and help her sit down.

She started crying. "She's gone, Mrs. Scuffer. Momma's gone to her heavenly home. She left us about three o'clock this morning. I came to tell you."

"I'm so sorry, Jetta Mae. I'm so sorry."

I'd never seen Jetta Mae cry. A lump rose in my throat. I dropped to my knees and grabbed her hand.

"It's hard, real hard," Jetta Mae said. "She fought so long, but now she's free of her pain. She was ready."

I wondered how Jetta Mae could know she was ready, but I knew better than to ask that question.

"What can we do to help?" Mom sat by Jetta Mae and rubbed her back.

"I feel bad, Mrs. Scuffer. My head's throbbing and my throat hurts every time I swallow." Mom rested her hand on Jetta Mae's forehead. "I hope I'm not getting what Momma had."

"Why, you're burning up," Mom said. "I'm calling Dr. Carter right now and will take you to see him."

THE END OF THE SIDEWALK

I'd never seen Jetta Mae sick before. Maybe she'd gotten what her mom had. "I'm sorry you don't feel good" I said. "You gotta get well." I rubbed her hot hand.

"I'll be okay. Just got a little hurting." She laid her head down on the table.

"Come on," Mom said. "Dr. Carter says he'll work you in."

Mom helped Jetta Mae to the car and told her to get in the front seat. Jetta Mae hesitated. I slid in beside Mom and patted the seat. Jetta Mae sat down next to me. Once, Aunt Liz told Sarah Jane that Negroes weren't supposed to ride in the front seat. I didn't see why it made a big difference, especially with Jetta Mae. Mom had her own set of rules now.

At Dr. Carter's office, Jetta Mae got out and went to the back of the building.

"Where's she going, Mom?" We sat in the waiting room in the front. There were a few white people there.

"All public places like doctors' offices and waiting rooms at bus and train stations have separate entrances. That's what the Freedom Riders are trying to change."

"Even Dr. Carter? I thought he liked everybody."

"Well, he's doing what everyone does now."

After a while, I asked, "Can I go check on Jetta Mae? She should be done by now."

Mom was reading a religious book called *The Screwtape Letters*. "I guess so, but come right back."

I left the waiting room and ran around to the back of the building where I saw a sign on the door that said *Colored Entrance*. Opening the door to a small room with wall-to-wall chairs, I didn't see Jetta Mae or anyone else. I tiptoed up to the desk like I needed to be quiet.

"Do you know if Jetta Mae is with Dr. Carter?" I asked the lady sitting at the typewriter. Her curly red hair sprouted from a bun on top of her head like a plant. She wore glasses and peered over them as she looked at me. Then she glanced down at the paper in front of her.

"She's with Dr. Carter now," she said. "He's been busy this morning. You better go back to the front waiting room. You're not supposed to be back here."

When I got back to the front waiting room, I looked around and didn't see one other person waiting. The doctor must have been busy with the white people.

After a while, Mom was told Jetta Mae would be done shortly, and we went around back to meet her. When she came out, Jetta Mae said, "Dr. Carter's a fine doctor, yes, he is. He gave me a shot and told me to stay with my sister tonight. He let me use his phone to call her. If I'm not better tomorrow, he wants to see me again. I might have a touch of pneumonia."

"I'm glad you don't have to go to the hospital," I said.

We left, and soon Mom turned down Lilly Street near Dr. Carter's office, the street where Jetta Mae's sister Cornelia lived. The paved narrow street had no sidewalks like ours. The yards had a patch of grass here and there. Mom pulled in front of the house at the end of the street.

"Thank you, Mrs. Scuffer. I appreciate it so much," said Jetta Mae.

I jumped out of the car. Mom and I each held one of Jetta Mae's arms as she walked in slow motion up to the door. Cornelia opened the door to help her inside.

"Call me and let me know how you're feeling tomorrow," Mom said. "I'll take you back to Dr. Carter if you need to go.

THE END OF THE SIDEWALK

I'll let your dad know too. Geneva is with him, so don't you fret about it now."

As we turned onto Woodrow Wilson Boulevard, a black and white police car came up behind us with its lights flashing. Mom pulled over and stopped. A policeman came to the car window and asked for her license.

"Mrs. Scuffer, what are you doing driving around in this neighborhood?" he asked as he looked at her license and wrote something down. Was he giving Mom a ticket?

"I dropped off my housekeeper at her sister's house. She's sick, and I took her to the doctor."

"Scuffer . . . you're the one on that Civil Rights Commission. Are you trying to stir up trouble?"

"I'm on the commission, but I'm not trying to stir up trouble. I want to promote equal rights for all people." Mom acted calm and talked like she would to anybody. I'd be stuttering up a storm if I were talking to the policeman. I gripped the door handle as if it could protect me. After seeing the police arrest the Freedom Riders, could he arrest Mom and me for driving in that neighborhood?

"Well, lady, remember this is Mississippi, and we have certain laws about segregation. You best stay on your side of town. People around here don't like your ideas. You need to be careful." With that, he put his hand on his holster, walked back to his car, slid inside, and slammed the door.

"He must have followed me," Mom muttered to herself, but I heard her as she pulled off and started toward home.

"Why would he do that?" I asked, pulling on my stringy ponytail.

"What?" She looked at me as if she didn't know what I was talking about.

"Why would that policeman follow you?"

She didn't say anything at first. She stared straight ahead and cleared her throat. I looked out the window to see if I noticed any more policemen around. We rode by Livingston Lake. I thought about the times we'd been swimming there in the summer. Only white people were allowed to swim there, even though there was a Black neighborhood right across the street.

"Many white people don't like the Civil Rights Commission," Mom said. "They want to keep things segregated. They don't want to treat Negroes right. I believe we should work together no matter what color we are."

"Is that why he said you need to stay on your side of town?"

"Yes. They won't let Negroes buy houses in white neighborhoods, or even have jobs in some stores."

"I bet they don't know that Jetta Mae lives right close to our neighborhood."

"Yes, they know that neighborhood is there, but they wouldn't allow them to live on our street," Mom replied.

"I wouldn't care if Jetta Mae lived right next door to us. I think that would be fun."

Mom smiled as she pulled up in the driveway. "That would be nice, wouldn't it?"

CHAPTER 6

WHRRRRR. Mom's sewing machine sat on the dining room table as she sewed a dress for Jetta Mae's mom. The pink material felt as soft as a baby blanket. Jetta Mae had told Mom that pink was her mom's favorite color. The funeral was tomorrow so Mom had to finish it. She'd worked on it for several days.

Aunt Liz came inside with a plate of her chocolate chip cookies, and Sarah Jane carried a gelatin salad. "Will you take these tomorrow?" Aunt Liz said.

I took the dish from Sarah Jane and motioned for her to come into the kitchen with me. She shook her head and said nothing.

"Aren't you going to the funeral?" Mom asked as she stopped sewing.

"No, I'm not comfortable about going," Aunt Liz replied.

"Good grief, it's Jetta Mae's mother." Mom frowned as she resumed sewing.

"Our town's in a mess right now. Jetta Mae doesn't expect us to come."

"Jetta Mae's been with us for nine years. I'm not concerned about what people think. I'm going to support her."

"You should be concerned. You're making a lot of people angry. The laws are in place whether you like it or not. I heard about the fire engine coming to your house. The whole neighborhood's talking about it. I'm not going to be involved."

With that, Aunt Liz and Sarah Jane walked out the door. Sarah Jane looked at me, but I couldn't tell how she felt. I thought she might have said something to me, but she'd just stood beside Aunt Liz like we were strangers. I wanted to cry. Sarah Jane and I had known each other since we were babies. When her dad had died in Korea, they'd lived with us for over a year until Aunt Liz found a house for them. I tried to tell myself that the reason she didn't talk to me today was because I was on restriction. She might be, too, for all I knew. It didn't make me feel a bit better.

"Mom, are you mad at Aunt Liz?" I looked at her hard to read her expression.

"No, but we're not in agreement right now. I've finished the gown for Mrs. Green and need to take it over to Jetta Mae."

I noticed she'd changed the subject, which meant she wasn't going to talk to me about Aunt Liz. I knew better than to ask any more questions right now, but I would talk to her about it later.

"May I go with you?" I'd never been to Jetta Mae's house.

"All right, but I'm not going to stay." Mom folded the pink dress and put it in a box.

I'd missed Jetta Mae. She hadn't come back to work yet. We drove down the street to her house. In her neighborhood, the houses were smaller than our house, which I considered normal sized. Her tidy house sat at the end of the road, and on the porch by the door sat a big washtub filled with dirt and red geraniums. Jetta Mae loved flowers. I knew she must have planted them.

When she opened the door, I went and wrapped my arms around her. She hugged me right back. I couldn't imagine what it was like to lose your mother. Mom handed her the box with the dress in it. She opened it and touched it.

"Lord, Mrs. Scuffer, this is so beautiful. I don't know how to thank you. You make my heart strings tingle." Tears rolled down her face as Mom gave her a hug.

"I was happy to do it," Mom said. "We'll see you tomorrow."

"Bless you. Thank you so much."

On the way home, I stared out the window at the small houses. "I'm glad I know where Jetta Mae lives. I didn't know what her house looked like."

"It's hard for Negroes to earn enough money for nice houses. Mr. Green wants to move out by Cornelia, but there aren't any houses available right now. Jetta Mae and her family have lived here a long time."

"Did you know Jetta Mae wants to have her own bakery one day?"

"No. When did she tell you that?" Mom glanced at me.

"I was telling her about wanting a horse and asked her what she wanted. That's what she said. A bakery. It would be the best in town."

"I agree. I never realized she thought about that."

My mind wandered to the funeral and what it would be like. Would Joseph and I be the only children there? I hoped the police wouldn't follow us again.

CHAPTER 7

MOM WORE her Sunday black dress and a wide-brimmed hat with her soft, dark hair curling around her face. I ran my fingers through my dishwater-blond ponytail. My black patent leather flats squeezed my big feet. Grabbing *Misty of Chincoteague*, I tucked it under my arm. As we walked out the front door, Joseph scooted by me with a basketball in his hand and bounced it down the steps. His blond hair was slicked down to his head like it had glue on it

"Son, go put that back in the house now." Dad had perspiration running down his face because of the steamy, hot weather. He tossed his Panama hat onto the front seat of the car and ducked his head as he got in. Dad was over six feet tall, and he wore size fourteen shoes. I must have gotten my big feet from him. A handsome man, his smile made anyone want to smile back.

"Mom, will we be the only white people at the funeral?" I asked. This being my first funeral, I didn't know what to expect.

"I don't know. It's possible. We're there to support Jetta Mae."

"Where will we sit? Can I sit with Jetta Mae?" I knew I would like to sit with her since I wouldn't know anybody else there.

"No, you can't sit with Jetta Mae. Her family will be seated together at the front. Someone will show us where to sit."

Mom didn't seem like anything was out of the ordinary, but I rubbed my sweaty palms together and looked around to make sure the police weren't following us. Dad drove into the church parking lot. The small church had a steeple with a cross on top. Two men, dressed in suits, stood on either side of the double doors.

"Now, Gertrude, you and Joseph stay close and follow us," Mom said. She needn't worry. Venturing off by myself hadn't crossed my mind. I'd never been to this church.

We walked up the steps to Blessed Deliverance Baptist Church. Dad took off his hat as he walked in the doorway. He nodded his head at the man who handed us each a fan with a picture of Jesus on the front and the words *Harvey Funeral Home* written in Christmas-tree green on the back. I couldn't tell what Dad thought about coming. He'd been quiet on the way over.

I kept my eyes looking straight ahead, but I didn't see any other white people out of the corners of my eyes. A man led us to the second pew of the church. Joseph walked down the aisle like he was the ring bearer in a wedding, looking from side to side and smiling at the people. Some smiled back at him. A "Reserved" sign hung on the side of the pew. Did they save this row for us, or for any white people who came? Did anyone wonder why we came?

I'd never seen a dead person before. The open casket sat right in front of the pews. I saw the tip of Mrs. Green's nose and her hands folded on top of the pink dress.

"Come with me." Mom took my hand and guided me up to the casket with Dad and Joseph behind us.

I stared at Mrs. Green's pasty brown skin, her closed eyes, her lips outlined with red lipstick, and her cheeks highlighted with rouge. Why did they put makeup and fancy clothes on a dead person when they were going to bury her in the ground? It gave me the heebie-jeebies. When we returned to the pew and sat down, I rubbed my clammy hands on my dress.

"She looked like she was asleep," Joseph whispered, tugging at my arm. "How do they know she's dead?"

"Because she quit breathing." I pulled on the waist of my dress, hoping to make it feel more comfortable. I could feel sweat running down my back.

The congregation stood as Jetta Mae and her family walked up the aisle to the casket. Each family member placed a rose right on top of Mrs. Green's pink dress and then kissed her on the cheek. Thank goodness we didn't have to kiss her. I shifted my weight from one foot to the other, but my feet still hurt. My legs wobbled like they were made of rubber. I thought I might faint.

I fanned my face like crazy and then sat down to steady myself. Mom shook her head disapprovingly and motioned for me to stand back up. She didn't seem to realize that I was dizzy. The open windows didn't offer much relief from the heat and neither did the fan. Grabbing the edge of the pew, I tried to think of other things, but my eyes and thoughts remained on Mrs. Green adorned with roses. Two men walked up, closed the casket and everyone sat down as the preacher walked to the podium. They didn't have an altar like our church.

"Let's rejoice as Maybelle Green walks through those pearly gates," the preacher said as he waved his arms up in the air. Did some white people think there were two gates in Heaven like the two water fountains at the zoo? I felt sure there was only one gate.

"Maybelle was right with the Lord," a man shouted. Several amens rang out.

"Hallelujah!" another shouted.

THE END OF THE SIDEWALK

This church had different rules than the church we attended. We had to be quiet when the preacher talked. When we said amen, we only said it together at the end of our prayers.

The people all started clapping, stomping their feet, and singing "When the Saints Go Marching In." It seemed more like a party than a funeral. Mom clapped along, even though at our church she would tell me to be reverent. Joseph jumped up and down, clapping and smiling. Dad didn't clap, so I didn't either. He wiped sweat from his face with his handkerchief.

When the service was over, the congregation gathered in the cemetery right behind the church under a green canopy tent with *Harvey Funeral Home* written on the flap. After a short prayer and Bible reading, everybody got in a circle around Jetta Mae and her family. They started singing "What a Friend We Have in Jesus." Many stood with their arms around each other, swaying as they sang. Mom sang her heart out like an opera star. Jetta Mae and her dad wiped tears from their eyes.

After the song, Mom walked over to Jetta Mae and hugged her for a long time. I stood by her looking down at the ground. When I looked up, I didn't see anyone paying attention to the white lady and Colored lady hugging like they couldn't let go of each other. Then it was my turn.

"Jetta Mae, I'm so sorry about your mom." I hugged her as tight as I could.

"She's in a better place now. Yes, Lord, no more pain or suffering. She's with Jesus." She squeezed me tight, then hugged Dad and Joseph. "Will you please stay for lunch? There's plenty of food."

"We'd love to," Mom spoke for all of us. I looked at Dad. He leaned over and whispered something to Mom. She nodded and he took Joseph and walked off. I wanted to follow them, but Mom waved to me to join her. As we got our plates, Mom sat down with a group of ladies. I stood there, not knowing where to go. A girl and two boys sat under a tree gobbling down their food. I walked over and sat down by myself, not far from them, trying not to look conspicuous.

"What's wrong? You think we have cooties?" one of the boys asked, nudging the other boy and giggling.

"No," I said. I started eating my food. I'd left my book in the car but wished I had it now.

The boys' black hair was in tight curls all over their heads. They almost looked like twins with starched white shirts and black pants. I didn't know what to say.

"You scared of us?" asked the girl as she picked up a drumstick and took a bite.

"No," I said and kept on eating. I didn't want to be rude, but I was scared. Well, maybe not scared, but uncomfortable.

"So, where you going to school? What grade are you in?" She was talking to me real friendly like.

"I'm going to Hardy Junior High, and I'll be in seventh grade." I pulled up some blades of grass and started making a little pile.

"I'm going to be in seventh grade, too, at Jim Hill Junior and Senior High," she said. "They're in the same building. My name's Latrella. Levar and Carl are going to be in eighth grade. Auntie Jetta works for your family, doesn't she?"

"Yes, she does. So, she's your aunt?"

"Not exactly. My grandma and her are cousins." Her friendly manner made me relax a little until one of the boys threw an acorn my way. I jumped. They giggled and ran off.

"Stop, Levar. Get out of here," she hollered to them, then said to me, "Don't mind him. He doesn't mean any harm. What do you like to do?" She moved to sit down beside me. I hoped she couldn't tell how nervous I was.

"I like to read, and I like riding horses." I fidgeted with the hem of my dress.

"Well, I like to sing and cook. Do you have a horse?" she asked. She adjusted a barrette on one of the seven black braids on her head.

"No, but I really want one. Dad says they're too expensive. Maybe someday I'll get one."

"I don't know anything about horses. Daddy Green's got a mule, but nobody rides it. It pulls the plow for his garden. So, what's your favorite book?" Latrella said.

"*Donna and Thunder*. Have you read it?"

"I never heard of it, but I don't have many books, even though I like to read."

"You can check it out of the public library if it's not in your school library. I checked it out so many times, my aunt bought me a copy."

"Our school library doesn't have a lot of good books. I've never been to the public library. That's just for Whites. Some students from Tougaloo College got arrested for going in that library downtown. If I'd been with them, I wonder if they would have arrested me?" She stood up and brushed the grass off her dress. "I went to the college library at Jackson State with my dad, but I didn't see any books I liked."

I couldn't believe she'd never been to the public library. It was one of my favorite places. I guessed that the Jim Crow laws said they couldn't use our library either.

Joseph came running up. "Come on. Dad's ready to go."

"I've got to go," I said as I rushed to join Joseph.

"Wait. You didn't tell me your name." She started coming toward me.

"It's Trudy. Bye," I yelled and hurried off. I didn't find her hard to talk to like I thought it would be. I'd never talked to a Negro girl my age before.

As we got in the car, I grabbed my book. What if I couldn't go to the library? I think I'd be miserable. Aunt Liz said books were my window to the world, and I knew she was right about that.

A police car cruised by as we pulled in the driveway. Skipper barked in the backyard. Dad got out of the car and waved, but the policemen didn't wave back.

CHAPTER 8

THE NEXT MONDAY, Jetta Mae walked by me as I brushed my tears away and tried to not look her way.

"I'm getting ready to leave," Jetta Mae said. "Why don't you come walk with me?"

"Okay." Maybe Jetta Mae could cheer me up. I didn't want her to know I was feeling sorry for myself, but I was. Sarah Jane had given me the brush-off after a week of restriction. I thought she'd be as excited as I was to get together, but no, she was going shopping with Polly.

"What's troubling my girl? It can't be that bad."

"Sarah Jane has a new best friend. When I found out she was busy with Polly, I called one of my Girl Scout buddies, and she said her dad won't let her come over because he doesn't like what Mom's doing. I'm not going to have any friends."

"Listen to me. You'll have friends. Not everyone disapproves of what your mom is doing. You need to hold your head high and be proud of yourself and your mom, because my people have been held back too long. When folks get to know you, they'll like you for sure. Just wait until school starts." Jetta Mae always looked on the positive side of things.

"I double-dog dread school starting. It's so big compared to Poindexter and most of my friends are going to another junior

THE END OF THE SIDEWALK

high. Sarah Jane's going to be in eighth grade, so I won't be with her. Besides, she'll probably hang out with Polly." I kicked a pecan off the sidewalk. It was still in the green hull. Soon there would be plenty to pick up, then Jetta Mae could make her pecan pie. It was almost as good as her butterscotch pie. I'd rather think about pie than about school starting.

"Look at it like a new adventure," Jetta Mae said. "It's closer to your house. You'll get a fresh start with new friends and lots of fun activities. I bet you'll love it."

"I hope you're right. I hope to goodness it'll be better than I think."

We reached the end of the sidewalk where a path led into a wooded thicket to her road.

"Now run home and remember not to worry about school," Jetta Mae said.

"See you tomorrow. Thanks for the pep talk."

"You're welcome as rain," she said and disappeared through the woods.

As I turned to leave, a shadow passed in the trees. I took a few steps closer and squinted. Someone was there. Latrella's head popped out from behind a tree.

"Come here for a minute," she whispered. I checked to make certain there was no one around, and I scooted into the wooded area. She motioned for me to follow her, and we went behind a couple of big bushes.

"Remember me from the funeral? I come here all the time. This is my thinking place. Nobody can see us back here. My granny lives right back there." She pointed toward the other side of the woods and smiled at me. I could see she had pretty teeth, not like mine with a space between them like a fence missing a slat.

"You still scared of me?" she said as she moved closer to me. She wiggled her bare feet, twirled around, then plopped on the ground, pulling her loose yellow dress down over her knees. I stood there trying to relax.

"No." I smiled. I didn't want to be rude, but Aunt Liz had told Sarah Jane we shouldn't socialize with Colored people. However, I wanted to talk with Latrella. No one would have to know.

"Say, can I borrow that book you told me about?" she said. "You know, the one about the girl and her horse? Come on and sit down with me." She reached out to grab my hand.

I didn't mean to, but I jerked it away because she surprised me. "What's wrong?" Her smile faded. She started to get up.

"Wait. You startled me, that's all. You can borrow *Donna and Thunder*. I'll bring it to you tomorrow, or I'll give it to Jetta Mae if I can't come. Do you live close to Jetta Mae?"

"I live with my mom and dad a few streets over, but I spend lots of time with my granny, Big Mama. Her house is right past the little store. Auntie Jetta's is back down the road."

"You have any brothers and sisters?" I asked.

"I have an older brother, Douglas. He's fifteen. My mom works at Jackson State as a secretary, and my dad's a math professor. Big Mama, she's the best. I stay with her as much as I can."

"I better go. I'll try to bring that book to you. Meet me here at nine tomorrow morning. If I'm not here after five minutes, then it will mean I couldn't come." I got up and brushed off my shorts.

"Okey dokey," she said and then took off running through the woods.

THE END OF THE SIDEWALK

Taking a quick peek when I walked back to the end of the path and seeing no one, I stepped out of the trees and ran home as fast as I could. Dad always told us to not go past the end of the sidewalk. Our street extended about a half a mile further to Lynch Street with houses on either side. He set that boundary because it separated the white neighborhood from the Negro neighborhood, but that was when we were little. The woods went back a long way from the sidewalk, and they were at the end of the sidewalk, not past it. I tried to make it okay in my mind to meet her. At least I would have a friend since Sarah Jane had Polly now.

CHAPTER 9

THINKING ABOUT what Jetta Mae had said about school being an adventure, I hopped on my bike for a ride to Hardy Junior High to check it out. The school stretched across a long block about half a mile from my house. The two story tan building was much bigger than my elementary school. It was closed, but I rode around in the back by the tennis courts and the gym. A big oak tree by the tennis courts seemed to be a good spot to sit and make a game plan. I'd brought my new book, *Misty of Chincoteague,* with me. I'd much rather think about horses than school and had already started reading it. I hoped one day I could go to Chincoteague and get me a wild horse to tame. I loved dreaming about it.

I glanced over at the tennis courts. It reminded me of the times Sarah Jane and I had played tennis. Maybe I could find someone else to play with since she had a new friend. I decided to head back home.

"Where have you been?" Mom asked as I came in the back door.

"I rode over and checked out the school. There's no one there now, but I saw the tennis courts and where the gym is. It's big. I'm nervous about school. I'm afraid people won't like me. I don't want people saying mean things about you and the Negroes."

"People will say all sorts of things about me, good and bad.

THE END OF THE SIDEWALK

We must stand up for what is right. Just smile as if they said something nice and walk away."

"Mom, I can't smile about that. It isn't funny and it isn't true. I don't want them saying mean stuff."

She walked over and put her arm around my shoulder. We sat down on the couch.

"I'm sorry. I know it's hard for you, but I'm not the only one who wants things to be different for the Negroes. Try to look for the good in people even if they have different ideas from you. Don't be upset because they see things differently."

"Like you and Aunt Liz?" I noticed Mom frowning.

"I think Liz and I think alike in most ways. She believes in equal rights, but our ways to approach things are different."

"I called Jenny from Girl Scouts, and she said she couldn't come over because her dad didn't like what you were doing."

"Listen, if you don't act like what other people say bothers you, then I bet they'll leave you alone. If they don't when school starts, I'll talk to their parents or the principal."

"No, Mom. I don't want you talking to anyone. That would only make it worse. Please don't do that."

"I won't unless you ask me to, but I don't want you to be afraid of going to school. You've always loved school."

"I know, but I went to the same school for six years. Now everything will be different, and I'll have several teachers instead of one. The same people won't be in each class. I don't know if I'll like that. Jetta Mae said to look at it as an adventure."

"She's right. You'll have an opportunity to meet more people and you'll have your own locker for your books and other things you don't want to carry around all day."

"I hope it will be like that. Were you ever nervous about school?"

"Not that I remember, but everybody's different. I think you'll find it to be good."

"I'll do my best." But I'd rather think of anything but starting school. At least she knew how I felt.

CHAPTER 10

THE NEXT DAY, I remembered my promise to Latrella to loan her *Donna and Thunder*, so I sneaked out the back door. I wouldn't stay long, but I wanted to keep my promise. My heart thumped in my chest. When I reached the end of the sidewalk, I dashed into the woods. At first, I saw no sign of Latrella. Then I heard a giggle. She stepped out from behind a large oak. I smiled, but I still felt uneasy. She was barefooted and wore a loose-fitting orange jumper. Her hair, no longer in neat braids, stood out all over her head. My hair had no pouf to it. It lay flat and limp against my head.

"Did I scare you?" she said. "Why are you so jumpy?"

"I wasn't sure if you would come." I shuffled my feet in the dirt.

"Heck, yeah. I can't wait to read that book. Let's go to the bushes," she said as she moved closer to me. We walked over to where we were before and both sat down.

"I went over to check out the school yesterday. I'm all jittery about starting school. I'm scared of boys. I don't know what to say to them."

"Shoot. I'm not scared of boys. If someone picks on me, I turn my nose up and priss right off. Big Mama says I need to act proper, but I won't let anyone get the best of me."

"I wish I felt like you."

THE END OF THE SIDEWALK

"You stick with me, and I'll help you get over that," she said, standing up in front of me with her hands on her hips like she was the boss of the universe.

"Here," I said, handing her the book. With a big grin on her face, she acted like I was giving her a piece of gold. She took my hand, pulled me to my feet, and threw her arms around me, hugging me hard. I hated to be skittish, but I couldn't help looking over her shoulder to see if anyone could see us.

"I'd better go since no one knows where I am," I said. "Maybe we can meet here next Monday afternoon at four? Let's keep it a secret, though. I think it's better not to tell." If anyone found out, I'd be on restriction again.

"Okay, thanks. See ya," she said as she tucked the book under her arm and ran back through the woods. I skedaddled back to the house.

When I got home, Mom was on the phone. I walked by her, and she smiled at me and pointed to the phone, showing me to not interrupt her.

"Hey, Trudy," Joseph yelled as I ran down the steps to the backyard. He threw a ball at me, but I missed it. I picked it up and threw it back. Of course, he caught it.

"You want to play catch?" he asked.

"Okay, but just for a few minutes."

For about ten minutes, we threw the ball back and forth. He caught the ball almost every time, and I missed it almost every time. I ran after several of his pitches that I missed. When I caught it, he would yell, "good catch," and he never complained when I missed it. He would have continued for an hour, I guessed, but I had some heavy thinking to do and stopped.

I headed straight for Miss Magnolia, my favorite tree. It used to be the meeting place for Sarah Jane and me, but now I didn't know if she'd join me anymore. The shiny broad leaves shielded me from the hot sun. As I climbed up on a low branch and leaned against the trunk, my body relaxed. Why couldn't I feel like this all the time? I loved the calm that washed over me like a wave pushing its way over the sand. I was hidden from view, and I could plan, think, and dream.

"Thanks, Miss Magnolia for a few minutes of quiet." I wished I felt relaxed about starting school. I called out to Joseph, "Hey, come here a minute. I want to talk to you." I wanted to find out how he felt about school.

He tossed his ball in the air, and it dropped to the ground before he came over to Miss Magnolia. "What's up?"

"Are you nervous about school starting?" He looked at me puzzled, as if he had no idea what I meant.

"Heck no. I can't wait to see all my friends. Why would I be nervous?" He picked up his ball.

"I don't know. Because of Mom being on the commission, you might get bullied."

"Nope, I haven't even thought about it. You worry too much. Come on, let's go over to Aunt Liz's." He started running.

I climbed down from Miss Magnolia and followed him, hoping Sarah Jane would talk to me some more about school, but she and Polly sat on the front porch. I started to turn around so I wouldn't have to deal with Polly, but I really wanted to patch things up with Sarah Jane. Joseph ran into the house to see Frank.

"Hi, what are y'all doing?" I said. I stood on the steps wishing Sarah Jane would invite me to join them.

"Not much. Mom's going to take us to the park in a few minutes." Sarah Jane glanced over at Polly, but I couldn't read her expression.

"I rode over to Hardy to check it out."

"No one's there yet," Polly chimed in, "and I don't think they want anyone there when the school isn't open."

"I didn't stay long and just rode around by the tennis courts," I said.

"If any teachers were there and saw you, they would tell you to leave," Polly replied.

An awkward silence followed and then Aunt Liz came out the door with Joseph and Frank behind her.

"Come on, girls. I need to pick up some things from the store on the way back."

She breezed by me and slid into the driver's seat looking as if she had a lot on her mind.

Sarah Jane and Polly ran to the car along with Joseph and Frank. "Bye, Trudy," they yelled and jumped in the back seat. They didn't even invite me to go. Hurt to my very core, I waved and ran home as fast as I could.

Jetta Mae stood at the clothesline hanging out some sheets and towels. She always said sun-dried was the best. I brushed my tears away and tried to use a brave voice. "Here, hand me a towel and I'll help you. Sarah Jane and Polly went to the park, and they didn't even invite me. Frank and Joseph went too."

"Don't trouble your heart with little stuff." Jetta Mae smiled at me. "Look on the bright side and find good in each situation. See, now you can help me. You know, Dr. Martin Luther King, he's got the right idea. He goes around trying to promote fairness in a peaceful manner. He has a beautiful way of talking the truth," she said while nodding her head.

"He's the one you said led the bus boycott," I said. "I'd like to hear him talk. What happened to the Freedom Riders in Alabama was awful. I'm glad you told me about him and Rosa Parks."

We walked together back into the house.

CHAPTER 11

THE PHONE RANG as we came in the door. Jetta Mae had the laundry basket, so I ran to answer the call.

"Scuffer residence, Trudy speaking." I heard deep breathing, but no one said a word. "Hello, may I ask who's calling?" There was more deep breathing. "Who's this?" I said, nervous about what I heard.

"Trudy, your mother's nothing but trouble," a muffled voice said.

"No, she's not." I hung up the phone like Dad had instructed us to do, but my hand shook.

"Who was that?" Jetta Mae asked. She set up the ironing board and waited for an answer.

"Oh, it was one of those mean calls. Dad said to hang up."

No matter what the man had said, I found it rattled my nerves. I went down the hall to my room, and I searched my desk for some paper and a pen. Then I sat down to compose a letter to that mayor who said such mean things to Mom.

Dear Mr. Mayor,

I don't know you, and you don't know me or my mother. The letter you wrote to my mom was rude. The things you said in your letter were not true. I am her daughter, and I am proud of her. You are a mayor. Don't you want equal rights for all the people in your town?

I know one Negro person, and she is smart and kind. My mom has lived in Jackson for a long time, so she certainly can help whoever she wants to help. Please don't write mean things anymore.

Sincerely,
Trudy Scuffer,
the proud daughter of June Scuffer

I folded the letter and went into Mom's room to get an envelope, stamp, and the address of the mayor. I hoped Mom wouldn't mind that I wrote to him. I shouldn't have read the letter, but it was in plain view on her desk. I took my letter to the black metal mailbox that hung on the front of our house right under our address numbers. I put the little red flag up. The mailman would pick it up.

I glanced at the red fire hydrant that stood at the curb in front of our house. I'd always tell my friends they couldn't miss my house because it was the one with the fire hydrant in front. Now I wished it wasn't there. I didn't want people to know where I lived.

When Mom came home, I told her about the call but not the letter.

"Well, I'm not in trouble," she said. "You did the right thing to hang up."

I knew she would say that.

At supper, Joseph piped up about going to the park with Frank. He was rattling on about it. I looked down at my plate while I ate because I didn't want Dad to see me upset.

"That sounds like fun," Dad said and then looked over at me. "Did you go, Gertrude?"

"No, I stayed here with Jetta Mae." I hoped he wouldn't ask why.

Joseph answered for me by saying, "Polly went with Sarah Jane."

Joseph and I cleared the table. It was my turn to wash the dishes. He'd dry them, and we'd put them away together.

"You should have gone with us," he said as we stood at the sink. "We got to ride the little train and swing on those big swings."

"Well, I wasn't invited. I wanted to go."

"Aunt Liz asked why you didn't come with us, and Sarah Jane said you had something else to do. I didn't know what you said to them, so I didn't say anything."

"Why, that's an outright lie. I never said that to them. I'm going to set things straight with her tomorrow." Then I overheard Mom talking to Dad, and I moved over by the refrigerator to hear better.

"Where're you going?" Joseph asked.

"Shhh," I said and put my finger to my lips. Mom was talking.

"The commission heard a case today where a white man moved his fence twenty yards onto this Negro man's property, then claimed it as his property. He stole over an acre of the Negro man's farmland."

"What happened?" asked Dad.

"Nothing, yet. They went to the courthouse, and the white man had submitted new deeds with the new boundaries. The clerk told the Negro man his papers were no longer legitimate. I hope when we present this information to Washington, they'll send someone to investigate these injustices." Mom hit the table with her hand. "It's deplorable how they're being treated."

I jumped and ran back to the sink but could still hear Dad's deep voice say, "It'll be a long time before things change here. Too many people are dead set in their ways, even the governor. You aren't going to change his mind or theirs."

I didn't hear what Mom said, but I'd heard enough. Dad kinda talked like Aunt Liz in saying that things weren't going to change.

Even though it was hot when I crawled into bed, I got up and shut my window. Skipper would bark if someone came into the backyard, but I felt safer with the window closed. The attic fan was on, but it didn't help much since my window was closed. I was sweating under my sheet, so I got up and cracked my window just enough to let some air in. I got out my diary and wrote down a plan.

Dear Diary,

I'm going to save my money to get horseback riding lessons.

I'm going to talk to Sarah Jane about lying.

I'm going to talk to Latrella about her friends.

Love, Trudy

The next morning, I heard Jetta Mae in the kitchen talking to someone. I pushed the swinging door, and Latrella stuck her head out from behind Jetta Mae.

"Bet you didn't expect me," she said. She was barefooted, her hair was back in seven neat braids, and she wore a pretty blue jumper.

"No, I didn't. How'd you get to come?"

"Big Mama had to go somewhere, so I begged Auntie Jetta to let me come, and here I am." She twirled around in a circle and laughed. "Auntie Jetta asked your mom yesterday if I could come with her for a few hours, and she said it'd be fine."

Mom hadn't mentioned anything to me, so I was completely surprised. "Did you tell Jetta Mae we met in the woods?" I whispered in her ear.

"No, I didn't, but she wouldn't care. Is your mom here?" She sat on her knees in a chair with her elbows on the kitchen table, peering into my face with her dark eyes.

"Nope. She's at another meeting. She's gone almost every day." I sat down too. My sweaty legs stuck to my chair. I tried sitting on my knees like Latrella, but it wasn't comfortable at all.

"What kind of meeting?" she asked.

"Oh, it's about civil rights for Negroes. She's working with some of the Negro leaders and some other white people to help Negroes register to vote and get things fair for them."

I told Latrella about the prayer meeting and how the fire truck came. She jumped up.

"I wish I could have been at her prayer meeting. Big Mama says my prayers are so strong they go right up through the roof to Heaven. She and I lie in bed when I spend the night with her, and we pray out loud." Latrella raised her hands toward the ceiling and said, "Amen."

I said, "Amen." Then I grabbed her hand.

"Come on, I want to show you something." Latrella followed me down the back steps, and I led her to Miss Magnolia. Since Sarah Jane was all caught up with Polly, I could share Miss Magnolia with my new friend.

THE END OF THE SIDEWALK

"Miss Magnolia, meet my friend Latrella," I said.

We climbed up, and Latrella patted the branch she sat on. "Glad to meet you. I'll give you a hug too."

"Miss Magnolia's my special tree. I come here all the time."

"Your tree's like my thinking place. It's kind of quiet and private. I like to sit and listen to the birds."

"Me too. Sometimes I come out and watch the sun come up. My cousin Sarah Jane and I meet here all the time. She lives over there on the next street." I pointed in the direction of her house.

"I'd like to meet her. Why don't you call her?" She looked out from the tree to see if she could see Sarah Jane's house.

"Uh, I don't think her mom will let her come over now. She's upset about us going to see the Freedom Riders." I didn't say that Aunt Liz would have a hissy fit if she saw me in the tree with Latrella.

"You tell her I'd like to meet her sometime, okay?" She grabbed a branch and jumped down to the ground. "You're a very nice tree, Miss Magnolia," she said and laughed as she wrapped her arms around the thick trunk.

I climbed down, and we went and sat on the white wooden swing together. Skipper sniffed at Latrella. She reached out and petted him.

"I wish I had a dog, but Mom and Dad say we're not home enough."

"I don't think Skipper's any trouble at all. I like taking care of him. I really want a horse though. I'm saving money so I can take lessons. Right up there on Claiborne Avenue, there's a pasture with two horses in it. If I got a horse, I might be able to keep it there. That's my dream."

"Do you know the people who own the horses?" she asked.

"No, but I think I'm going to get up my nerve and go meet them. Have you ever ridden a horse?"

"Nope, I never have. Have you?"

"Yes, I met a girl at Girl Scout Camp, and sometimes I go and ride with her. I've been about three times, and I love it."

She looked around my backyard and then she jumped out of the swing. "Did you know that a hundred years ago, this land we're living on was a plantation?"

"Are you serious?"

"I surely am. That's why there are so many pecan trees here. It had a pecan grove, and back there was a huge cotton field. My dad told me all about it. His great grandparents were slaves right here."

"I never knew that. I wonder what the plantation house looked like?"

"I don't know, but Dad said his grandmother told him those were hard times. They weren't even allowed to read, and they had to do whatever they were told to do."

"Wow, I'd be miserable if I couldn't read." I looked up at the trees and said, "They are pretty old, aren't they?"

"Yes, and I'm glad things have changed some, but it could be a lot better. My dad says most white people don't know what equal means."

"My mom thinks that, too, and she wants it to be equal for all. Let's go inside and play some cards. Do you know how to play Go Fish?"

"Sure do." We went inside and sat on the floor in my room. After shuffling the cards, I dealt them out and before long, she laid down four tens and said, "I'm out of cards. I have five books. How many do you have?"

"Three. You win." As I put the cards away, she looked around my room. "Is this your room all by yourself?"

"Yes. Joseph's room is down the hall."

"I have my own room at home, but when I stay with Big Mama, we sleep in the same room. Our beds are side by side, snug up tight. I like it, but sometimes she snores and wakes me up." She made a loud snoring sound, and we laughed.

"My dad snores so loud sometimes that I can hear him when I'm in bed. Oh, Mom's here. Come on, let's go see her."

We went in the kitchen where Jetta Mae was putting dishes away. Mom smiled and said, "Why, you must be Latrella. Jetta Mae's told me about you."

"Yes, ma'am," Latrella said. She acted a little shy, which surprised me. She folded her hands in front of her and said, "Pleased to meet you. Trudy and I met at the funeral. We had a good time today."

"Now we need to be getting on home," Jetta Mae said. "Stop all your rattling. Trudy's mom has lots to do." Jetta Mae pulled Latrella out the door. I followed them down the steps.

"You come again soon. I had fun today," I said.

"Maybe I can. Auntie Jetta says this was a special occasion," Latrella said. After she left, I wondered what Dad would say if he knew she'd come over.

Back in the house, I went to see Mom. "Latrella and I had fun today. Can she come again?"

"Mm-hmm." She wasn't even listening. She sorted the mail on the dining room table. Someone sent her the newspaper article with a picture of the commission. I picked it up and read it. The article stated that she was the only woman on the committee with four men, two white and two Negro.

"Can I ask you a question?" I said, fidgeting with my shirt. No use trying to talk to her about Latrella.

"Yes, of course." Mom looked up from her mail.

"Well, I was wondering if you would . . ."

"Would I what? I've a lot of letters to go through. Tell me what you want." She sounded exasperated.

"Would you take me horseback riding sometime?"

"We'll see. Not this week, though. I've got a full schedule." Mom shuffled some more of the mail, and I started down the hall.

I could ride the bus down to the stables if she would let me. Then I wouldn't have to wait for her to take me. I wished Katie would call again, but she lived way across town. I could call tomorrow, and we could plan to meet at the stable. I wanted to ride at least once before school started, but time was running out.

CHAPTER 12

THE NEXT DAY when the phone rang, I hesitated before answering it. I breathed a sigh of relief when I heard Sarah Jane's voice.

"Do you want to go see *The Parent Trap?*" she said. "Today is the last day it's playing. Mom said she would take us since we didn't get to see it on your birthday."

Surprised by her invitation, I hoped it meant we could make up before school started. "Sure, let me check with Mom." I ran to Mom's room, hoping maybe she would go with us.

Mom said I could go, but she had too much to do. I should have known that would be her answer. To my knowledge, she hadn't talked to Aunt Liz since she brought the food over for the funeral.

I ran over to Sarah Jane's, and lo and behold, there was Polly standing on the porch with Sarah Jane. I wouldn't be able to talk to Sarah Jane about what happened with Polly around.

Aunt Liz drove us downtown. After riding around the block, she found a space and parallel parked her Chevy near the theater. As we walked down the street, we heard yelling. In the doorway of a building, a Negro man crouched, covering his head.

A policeman yelled at the man, "Get up from there, you lazy, filthy scum. Don't you know you can't be hanging around here begging?"

The man got up and started stumbling down the street with his head down. I thought he was going to fall.

THE END OF THE SIDEWALK

"Aunt Liz, that policeman didn't have to talk so mean," I said.

Aunt Liz grabbed my arm. "Come on, girls. We don't want to miss the movie." She pulled us around the corner.

"But Aunt Liz," I said.

She frowned at me and said, "That's not our business."

"That man should follow the rules," piped Polly. Of course, she had to throw her two cents in.

At the theater, Aunt Liz scrambled in her purse to find the money for the tickets. She glanced around, then guided us into the theater.

"I felt sorry for that man, didn't you?" I whispered to Sarah Jane when we sat down.

"Yes," she said. At least I didn't get stuck by Polly.

"Shhh, the movie's starting," Aunt Liz said.

It was about two twins at a camp, and they didn't know each other. Their parents had divorced, and they grew up in separate towns. Hayley Mills played the part of both girls. They had used trick photography, but I couldn't concentrate on the movie. Sarah Jane leaned over toward me and said, "Does this movie remind you of us at Girl Scout Camp?"

"Sure," I agreed, but I wasn't enjoying the movie because I was thinking about that man.

Sarah Jane put some popcorn in her mouth and crunched it. She murmured something to Polly. Was I the only one worrying about that poor man we just saw? I kept looking at Aunt Liz to see if she was watching the movie or worrying like me. She didn't even look at me.

"How did you like the movie?" Polly asked when it was over.

"I thought it was great."

"Yeah, it was," I said half-heartedly. I peered around the corner as we walked back to the car, hoping to see that the man was all right, but I didn't see him or the policeman.

When they stopped at my house, I told them goodbye and thanked Aunt Liz and Sarah Jane for inviting me. Walking into the house, I wished I had stayed home.

Mom was sorting through her mail. "How was the movie?" she asked.

"Good. It reminded me of Girl Scout Camp. But something happened on the way that was terrible. We saw a policeman yell at this poor Negro man sitting by a store front. I felt sorry for the man, but Aunt Liz said that it wasn't our business and that we all must respect the laws."

"What?" Mom looked surprised.

"Well, the policeman said the man wasn't supposed to be sitting in the doorway of a building. He could have asked nicely for him to move. He didn't have to yell."

"I don't know what it's going to take for Negroes to be treated fairly," she said. "I'm sorry that happened. How did it make you feel?"

"I had a hard time concentrating on the movie because I kept thinking about that poor man."

"It's a shame someone can be so ugly to a poor Black man who probably has no place to call home."

"You're right, Mom." As I was leaving the room, I heard Mom say to herself, "I wish Liz would take a stand with me."

"I'm going out back," I said. Skipper lay under the tree by the garage. I grabbed my trusty book and headed out to visit Miss Magnolia. Skipper came running up to me, licking my hand and jumping around all over the place.

THE END OF THE SIDEWALK

"Skip, you're always glad to see me. You cheer me up. Wish you could talk." He lay down, and I rubbed his belly. "Our town's in a mess. The Freedom Riders have stirred everything up, and now everybody seems mad about it." I scratched his ears. "I start school soon, and I dread it. Sarah Jane's acting weird, and I don't want to be by myself with no friends." He licked my hand and panted as if he understood.

"Okay, boy, that's enough." Climbing up in Miss Magnolia, I settled on my branch and opened my book. I tried to read, but it was no use. It couldn't hold my attention. Skipper sat and looked up at me, panting.

I climbed down and patted his head. "You want to go for a walk?" He started turning in circles and barking. I snapped on his leash, and he pulled me through the yard. I thought I'd walk up to Claiborne and see the horses.

He saw a cat and started pulling me up the sidewalk. "Hold on, Skipper." I jerked the leash to make him slow down. The cat disappeared into someone's backyard, but he was still pulling. When we got to the fence, the horses started coming over until Skipper barked at them.

"Skipper, be quiet. I want you to meet them. They're so pretty." But he wasn't about to stop, so I had to turn around and go back home.

"Skipper, when I get a horse, you're going to have to be nice, or I won't take you to see it." He wagged his tail like he knew I was talking to him.

"I'm back, Mom." She was at her desk in her study. She looked up as I stuck my head in the door.

"Where'd you go? I didn't realize you'd left. I thought you

were out back." She picked up a letter, folded it, and stuffed it in an envelope.

"I took Skipper for a walk. We went to see the horses up on Claiborne."

"Go find Joseph and tell him it's time to eat."

At supper, she said to Dad. "I've got to go to Washington DC next week. If you must go out of town, I'll ask Jetta Mae to stay here for a couple of nights with the children."

"I'll look at my schedule," Dad said. The phone started ringing. "Here we go again. I've got a solution for this caller." He snatched a pillow off the chair in the living room, grabbed the phone off the receiver, hung up, took the phone off again, and put it under the pillow on the phone table so we couldn't hear the dial tone. "Now we can eat in peace."

I sat there mulling over what Mom had said before the phone rang. "If you aren't going to be here on the first day of school, then who'll take me?" I asked.

I wasn't a baby, but the first day of junior high seemed important to me. I wanted her to be around. It hadn't even entered her mind that school started next week.

"Your dad or Aunt Liz will take you, and then you and Sarah Jane can walk home after school." She didn't know that Sarah Jane had a new best friend, and Aunt Liz might not even want me around Sarah Jane anymore after what happened.

After supper, Mom picked up her plate and started walking into the kitchen as if leaving me next week was no big deal. "Gertrude, you better go practice your piano," she said. "I'll come in there in a minute and listen."

I frowned, still fretting about her going out of town, but

THE END OF THE SIDEWALK

Dad said, "Yes, play something for me."

"You know I can't play worth a toot."

He patted my shoulder and smiled. "Practice makes perfect."

I found a simple piece I already knew and started playing. Dad sat down in his chair, leaned back, and closed his eyes. When I stopped, he looked over and said, "Now, that sounded pretty good to me. Can you play one more? You might put me to sleep."

Mom slipped in and sat on the arm of Dad's chair. He held her hand. I wanted to play well for them both. I knew Dad was trying to make me feel better, so I picked out one more tune and played it. When I finished, he got up and said, "Keep up the good work. I enjoyed your concert."

"You are playing much better," Mom said.

"Thanks, Mom. I wish you didn't have to go out of town right on the first day of school."

"I know dear, but I don't set the dates for these meetings, and this one is important. You'll be fine, I'm sure."

I didn't think I would be fine.

When the timer rang, I jumped up, relieved that I was finished with my chore of piano practice. In my room, I tried once again to disappear into the world of *Misty of Chincoteague*.

The attic fan pulled in a breeze from outside, the crickets sang me to sleep, and Latrella met me in my dreams. She handed me my book, but she had a big bandage on her head. When I asked what happened, she said, "You know. Why didn't you help me?" She turned and ran back through the woods. When I tried to follow her, the woods never ended, and I lost sight of her. I was yelling "Wait, Latrella, wait," when I woke up.

CHAPTER 13

TROUBLED BY my dream, I had a hard time going back to sleep. I tossed and turned, but at some point, I must have drifted off because when I woke up, the sun shone through my window, and the birds chirped in the trees. I could hear Jetta Mae singing in the kitchen.

I rushed to dress and went into the kitchen to talk to her. The smell of the crisp bacon sitting on the table tickled my nose. I picked up a piece of toast and took a bite.

"You know what?" I said. "I've been thinking about how to go horseback riding. I could see if those people on Claiborne would let me clean the stalls and groom the horses. They might even let me ride one. I never see anyone riding them. I'd work for free if I could ride."

"Sounds like you got it all figured out, but you better run it by your parents," Jetta Mae said.

"What about your bakery dream? Have you made some plans?" I asked.

"No, I do think about it, but it's not something I can afford right now."

"You ought to have a bake sale and make you some money."

"You're full of ideas, aren't you?" Jetta Mae said, laughing.

Mom came into the kitchen. "Trudy, I'm going to McComb with Dr. Beittel to help with voter registration. I won't be back

THE END OF THE SIDEWALK

until about seven tonight. You help Jetta Mae all you can. She'll stay until your dad gets home."

"Yes, ma'am."

After she left, I asked Jetta Mae, "Have you ever met Dr. Beittel? He's president of Tougaloo College."

"No, I haven't had the pleasure. I'd like to meet him someday."

"Well, I'd like to meet him also. I think he's brave to be president of a Negro college, but I bet many people don't like him because of it. I'm glad he went with Mom to McComb."

I got an apple out of the refrigerator and went out back to get my bike. Joseph met me with a long worm wiggling in his fingers.

"Look what I found," he said. "Frank and I are collecting worms so we can go fishing."

"That looks like a good juicy one. Where are you going fishing?"

He dropped the worm in a jar that had dirt in it. "I'm going to ask Dad to take us somewhere."

"You want to go with me to see the horses? I'm taking this apple to my favorite one. He always comes right up to the fence. I named him Whisper."

"Not this time. Frank and I have a contest to see who can find the most worms. I better stick to this." He started digging again.

I got my bike and went out the gate, pretending like my bike was my horse. I pedaled as fast as I could, letting the warm air blow through my hair. Right past the high school was the pasture. The white split-rail fence extended all the way around the property. A long drive led up to the house with the barn off to one side. The horses were grazing in the pasture. I climbed up on the fence and held up the apple. Whisper looked at me and perked up his ears, then lowered his head and walked toward me. I didn't even have to call him. His brown coat glistened in the sun. He flicked his tail as he got closer to the fence. I balanced myself on the top rail and held the apple out. He took a large bite.

"Don't be greedy," I said and patted his nose. I laughed when he took the rest of the apple and chewed it up. I wanted more than anything to climb on his back, but I knew I couldn't. He came close to the fence and let me run my fingers through his mane.

"You're beautiful, you know that. I wish you were mine. I hope someday soon I can help take care of you. I'll come see you every day after school if I can." He nuzzled me and almost made me lose my balance. I grabbed the post and climbed down. "That's all I have today. See you, Whisper."

When I got home, I glanced at the clock and saw it was almost four. I realized that Jetta Mae wouldn't be leaving to go home at her regular time, and I was supposed to meet Latrella. I needed to hurry because I didn't want her to think I wasn't coming.

I grabbed *Misty of Chincoteague*. As I rushed out the door, I said, "Jetta Mae, I'll be back."

I ran down the sidewalk. Out of breath when I reached the end, I did a quick check behind me, then dashed into the woods. There sat Latrella with *Donna and Thunder* in her hand. I breathed a sigh of relief when I saw there weren't any bandages on her head. Latrella looked at her arm at an invisible watch.

"You're late. Where's Jetta Mae?"

"Mom's out of town, so Jetta Mae's staying until my dad gets home." My dream flashed before me as I looked at Latrella. I wondered if I was putting her life in danger by meeting her. I handed her *Misty of Chincoteague*. "This is different from the other book.

THE END OF THE SIDEWALK

This book is true, about wild ponies. I think I'd like to tame a wild horse. I might have a horse farm when I grow up."

"I'm going to be a doctor, but I want to read it anyway. I loved *Donna and Thunder*."

She looked at the book I had handed her, then she handed it back. "I better not take this one. It looks brand new."

"Don't be silly. I got it for my birthday, but I just finished reading it." I handed it back to her. "This afternoon I went up to see my favorite horse in that pasture on Claiborne. I pretend that his name is Whisper. He comes right up to the fence when he sees me."

"Can you ride him?" she asked.

"No, I don't know the people he belongs to. I don't ever see anyone riding him. I take him an apple or carrot each time I go. Maybe one day I'll have the nerve to go meet the people who live there."

"I'd go with you if I could, but I know that wouldn't be possible."

"I know. I want to be your friend, but I'm not sure we should meet here. Someone might see us and get us in trouble. I had a bad dream about you. You had a bandage on your head. You were mad at me, then ran away in a forest that kept going, and I lost you."

"I come here all the time, and no one ever sees me back in my corner of the woods. It's far enough from the path on the other end. Anyway, your dream was just that—a dream."

"I must go now. Maybe we could be pen pals. We could write letters to each other and hide them somewhere. I want us to be safe, but I want to be your friend."

"Let's write letters and still meet sometime," she said. "I'll come with Auntie Jetta as often as I can so I'd be the one who would be in trouble if we got caught." She grinned as she jumped around like a kangaroo.

"See, I don't want that for either of us," I said. "Writing letters sounds like a good plan. Where can we leave the letters?" We looked around in the woods and found a big rock. It took both of us to push it to a place that was right near a tree.

"You write first." She grabbed my hand and squeezed it. This time, I squeezed hers back.

CHAPTER 14

THAT EVENING when Mom got home, we were at the table eating supper with Dad. She fixed her plate and joined us. As usual, the minute she started eating, the phone rang. It was the caller who always called during supper, and we didn't answer. Once again, after the phone stopped ringing, Dad shook his head as he took the receiver off the hook and covered it with a pillow.

"That's someone with too much time on his hands."

If Mom heard him, she ignored it and said, "We registered eight people today. We were able to use the standard questions they use for white people. Often, they ask impossible questions and ask them to recite part of the Constitution of the United States. It's ridiculous. Mr. Herbert Lee, a member of the NAACP, said it was good they could register without being turned away. He thanked us for coming and helping."

Dad looked at Joseph. "What did you do today?" He obviously wanted to talk about something else.

"Frank and I found twenty worms. We want you to take us fishing. You want to see them?"

"Where are they?" Dad asked.

"In a jar in my room. I put lots of dirt in there with them and poked holes in the lid with your hammer and a nail."

"Well, I guess we'll have to get out our fishing poles this weekend."

THE END OF THE SIDEWALK

When supper was over, Mom and Dad went back to their room. I heard Dad raise his voice and say, "Do you want me to lose my job? Mr. Ross is on the White Citizens Council, and they see the commission and you as real troublemakers."

I ran to the hallway to see what was going on. I hated to hear Mom and Dad argue. Then the doorbell rang. Joseph ran to the door but stopped because Dad had a rule to not answer the door at night without asking who it was. By that time, Mom and Dad were there.

"Who is it?" Dad said.

I looked out the window and saw lights flashing. I thought it was the firemen again, but the voice behind the door said, "Police, sir."

Dad opened the door, and two policemen stood there, their handcuffs and billy clubs dangling from their belts and their guns in holsters on their belts. Were they going to arrest Mom? I grabbed my chest to try and stop my heart from beating so hard.

"What can I do for you?" Dad said. "Why do you have your lights flashing?"

"Well, sir, someone reported a disturbance here. We came to check. What kind of problem are you having?"

Dad shook his head. "There's no disturbance here. We just finished eating supper."

"Sir, we need to come in and check things out."

Dad put his hand on the door. I hoped he wouldn't slam it in their face, but he looked upset.

"Excuse me, but you can't come in here," Dad said. "We have young children, and they're already scared. It's unnecessary. Do you have a search warrant?"

Mom stood by Dad and took his hand, saying, "We're fine. Now please leave."

I ran over to Mom, and she put her arm around me. The faint scent of her perfume tickled my nose. I knew Mom could feel me shaking, but she held me tight. Dad put his arm around Joseph. We stood together as a family. The argument Mom and Dad were having earlier was forgotten. I saw Dad squeeze Mom's hand. I calmed down but I still felt uneasy.

"Please go and don't disturb us like this again," Dad repeated.

"Sorry to bother you, sir. We're just doing our job." The policemen backed down the steps, and Dad shut the door. He muttered under his breath something about another form of harassment. We all sat down on the couch together.

"Dad, what's a search warrant?" I held Mom's hand to make me feel safe.

"When police come to your house, you don't have to let them in unless they have an official paper that gives them permission. Someone who disapproves of your mom's position called them, I suppose."

"I wish they would leave us alone. Is this going to keep happening?" I started crying.

Joseph turned and peered out the window. "Me too. They scared the living daylights out of me."

"I'm sorry it scared you, but we're all okay," Mom said. "We may have to put up with other people's actions because they don't agree, but like I've said before, we must stand up for what is right." Mom hugged me and Joseph and then got up.

She went over and sat down at the piano, then started playing. Dad, Joseph, and I gathered around her. It eased the tension

THE END OF THE SIDEWALK

we all felt. She played "God Bless America." We all started singing. It had been a long time since we had done this as a family, and I loved it.

The phone rang, interrupting our song. Dad went to answer it saying, "It better not be another one of those crank callers." After a few seconds, he held out the phone receiver and said, "It's for you, Trudy."

I ran to get it, hoping it was Sarah Jane. Instead, the voice I heard made my heart jump. "Hi Katie," I said.

"I was calling to see if you could come ride on Saturday."

"I'd love to. I was just thinking about you today, and I was going to call. Let me ask my mom." I ran to Mom and begged her to let me go. She said she thought it would be fine.

Back at the phone, I said, "Sure, Katie. I'd love to. What time? Two o'clock? I can't wait. Thanks. I'll see you then." I hung up and went back to the living room, thinking the evening was ending a lot better than it had started.

That night I wrote in my diary.

Dear Diary

Most people want to stay segregated, but Mom wants to integrate. I liked things how they used to be, but now I'm beginning to see that change is hard. It's happening whether I want it or not. I get to go ride with Katie on Saturday. My dream to ride horses is coming true.

I then got some paper and started writing a letter to Latrella.

Nancy Schutt McCorkle

Dear Latrella,

You won't believe what happened tonight. The police came to our house and said someone had reported a disturbance. They wanted to come in, but my dad wouldn't let them because they didn't have a search warrant. That is a piece of paper that gives them permission, but they must have a good reason. It was scary. The good news is that Katie called, and I get to go ride a horse on Saturday with her. I wanted to share this poem with you. My English teacher read it to us last year, and I liked it so much, I asked her for a copy. My favorite line is the one about the rainbow holding out her hand. Let me know how you like it. Write me back. I'm glad we're friends.

I Meant to Do My Work Today
by Richard Le Gallienne

I meant to do my work today—
But a brown bird sang in the apple tree,
And a butterfly flitted across the field,
And all the leaves were calling me.
And the wind went sighing over the land,
Tossing the grasses to and fro,
And a rainbow held out its shining hand—
So what could I do but laugh and go?

Your friend,
Trudy

CHAPTER 15

THE NEXT DAY, I took my letter into the woods and put it under the rock. I wanted to talk to Latrella. I didn't dare try to talk to Sarah Jane about the police coming because she might tell Polly. Aunt Liz might find out too. It would only make things worse between Mom and her. Latrella and I didn't plan to meet today, but I needed to talk to someone.

When I reached the end of the sidewalk, I hesitated for a moment. If Dad found out, he would put me on restriction again for sure. I decided to chance seeing Latrella in person. It wouldn't take long. I rushed through the woods, and then there I stood in front of a store. An old man sat on the porch. He gripped a brown wooden cane and wished me a good morning. His hand shook, but I could tell it wasn't from fear of me. He had something wrong with his nervous system.

"It's going to be another hot one," he said. He wiped his head with a red bandana like the cowboys wear, then stuck it in his pocket. His hand trembled as he rubbed it on the farmer overalls he wore. His curly gray hair poked out from under a dusty brown hat. He smoked a pipe, and as he blew out a puff of smoke, the smell of tobacco filled the air.

"Hi, do you know Latrella?" I said. I went up the steps and reached for the handle of the screen door.

THE END OF THE SIDEWALK

"What did you say, child?"

I was about to chicken out and run back home, but I forced myself to open the door. A lighted Coke sign hung in the window. A cold Coke would taste good right now. My mouth felt like I had stuck a cotton ball in it.

"Never mind," I said and crept inside the dark store.

The shelves were crammed with cans and boxes of food. The narrow aisles made it hard to move without fear of knocking something over, much less get around someone else who might be leaning over to get a can of tomatoes. The lighted cases at the back of the store held the milk, juice, and other things that needed refrigeration. A white box freezer stood by the far wall with a picture of a Nutty Buddy on the outside. I walked over to peer inside and saw it was filled with Creamsicles, ice cream cartons, Popsicles, and ice cream sandwiches. I started to open it but realized I didn't have any money.

"Can I help you?" a lady with a white apron called out as she walked toward me. I decided I'd better skedaddle. Why would a white girl be looking for a Black girl?

"I'm just looking," I said and turned to run out the door. I bumped into someone who was leaning down to get something off the bottom shelf. She grabbed my arm to keep her balance.

"Excuse me, I'm leaving," I said.

"Lawsy me, Gertrude. What in the world are you doing here?" I stared at Cornelia Green, Jetta Mae's sister. I panicked. I hadn't anticipated running into anyone I knew. She'd tell Jetta Mae, Jetta Mae would tell Mom, and it would be restriction for me again, if not worse.

"Uh, I was looking at candy. Gotta go." I almost tripped getting out the door.

"Have a nice day and watch your step," said the man on the porch, but I didn't even reply.

Breathless by the time I reached home, I ran and climbed up Miss Magnolia to calm down before going in the house. I hugged her trunk to steady myself because I shook like I had fever chills. I took some deep breaths and said to myself. "Trudy, calm down. Stand up for what you believe."

But I wasn't sure where I stood. Being around Latrella had changed my thoughts. Why did we have to hide our friendship? It didn't seem fair to me. I wished I could talk to Sarah Jane about it, but I was afraid she wouldn't approve of Latrella and me meeting.

I decided to go over to Sarah Jane's anyway. I wouldn't tell her about last night, but we could talk about school starting. My nerves were like a rough saw blade, pointed and sharp, making my skin prickle.

Sarah Jane and Polly sat on her porch swing. I started to turn around and go home. They saw me and waved, so I couldn't very well change my mind.

Jealous thoughts swirled in my head. I shook my head trying to rid my mind of bad feelings. I wanted to like Polly, but all I could think was that she'd stolen my best friend.

"What have y'all been doing?" I asked as I sat down on the porch by the swing.

"Just talking about school and football games," said Sarah Jane. I noticed Polly staring at me. I looked down at my cowboy boots when I realized that her eyes were on them.

"What is it?" I said. "Go ahead and spit it out." I had to force myself to sit still. I wanted to streak out for home and be away from her forever.

THE END OF THE SIDEWALK

"You aren't wearing those to school, are you?" Polly said.

She's got some nerve, I thought. I was furious. My face heated up like a campfire. "For your information, I just might. Why would you care anyway? You're rude."

"I was going to give you some tips on school," Polly said, "but I can see you don't want any advice."

I jumped up and ran across the street, not looking back. I fought back tears. Sarah Jane hadn't even defended me. How could she like Polly? I dreaded going to school even more now. Who'd be my friend? I wasn't planning to wear my boots on the first day, but I might now to spite them both. I just needed nerve to do it. Why did I let Polly bug me so much?

CHAPTER 16

SATURDAY ARRIVED, and I couldn't contain my excitement. I imagined galloping through the woods on a horse. The thought filled my heart with joy. After putting on my jeans and my boots, I scrambled out to the car.

"Katie said to meet her at Miller Stables," I said to Mom. "Jinx is there because she went to a rodeo last weekend and left him there. She got a blue ribbon in barrel racing."

"That's wonderful. I didn't know that she competed." Mom handed me ten dollars to pay for the riding.

"Thanks, Mom. Do you know if Negroes have a stable where they can ride horses?"

"Not that I know of. Katie might know, but I doubt that they do."

"Latrella's never ridden a horse. It would be fun to go with her, but she couldn't ride at Miller's, I don't think."

"No, that would not be allowed now, but maybe someday. It's nice that you would think about her."

Katie stood outside the stable waving when we pulled up. "Bye, Mom. See you about five." I jumped out of the car and ran to give Katie a hug.

Katie already had Jinx saddled up, and I picked a pretty Palomino named Sandy. We set out on one of the trails that went

THE END OF THE SIDEWALK

by the Pearl River. The heat didn't bother me at all, and as we trotted along, a slight breeze cooled us. A great blue heron stood like a statue at the water's edge but took off as we passed by.

"Look at his wing spread," I said in amazement as he flew across the river.

Katie rode ahead of me. "I have another rodeo competition in two weeks. Would you like to go with me?"

"You bet I would. I've never been to a rodeo." I couldn't believe my ears. I had read about them in books.

"They're a lot of fun. They have lots of different events like cattle roping and barrel racing and steer wrestling. I only do the barrel racing."

"I can't wait to see you win. You must be speedy."

"Jinx loves to go fast. When we head back, we can do some galloping. We don't want to get the horses too hot."

"Do any Negroes compete?" I asked.

"Nope. I've never seen any. Sometimes there are Negro boys helping with the horses, but they aren't allowed to ride them."

"Do you think that's fair?" We rode side by side.

"I never really thought about it, but I guess if they wanted to ride, they should be allowed to. It's mostly boys and girls that live on farms or in the country."

"Are you prejudiced against Negroes?" I asked.

"What do you mean? I don't know any except our maid Sadie. I like her fine."

"I mean, if you knew a Negro girl, would you be her friend even if other people didn't want to be?"

"I guess I would. That's not likely to happen, though, because they have their own schools. Come on, let's gallop up to that clearing."

She kicked the sides of Jinx with her feet, and Jinx took off. It startled my horse, and he broke into a gallop following her. We raced up the hill, and when we reached the clearing, I was out of breath from excitement. I knew without a doubt that I wanted my own horse someday.

Katie jumped off Jinx and untied a bag from her saddle. She pulled out two drinks and some potato chips. I climbed off my horse, and we let them graze a little while we enjoyed the chips and drinks.

"Are you anxious about school?" I asked.

"No, not a bit. Are you?" She wrapped up the chips and stuck them back in the bag along with the empty bottles.

"I am a little. The school's so much bigger, and I'll have so many classes. There will be so many new people." I got the reins of my horse as we mounted back up.

"Oh, don't worry. You'll make friends easily. You're friendly and cute. I wouldn't worry," she said.

We started galloping down the hill, but my horse stepped in a hole and stumbled. When he reared up, I slid right out of the saddle and hit the ground hard. I landed on my right arm.

Katie came galloping back. She jumped off, kneeling beside me. "Are you okay?"

When I moved my arm to try and get up, a sharp pain shot through it.

"Ouch!" I screamed.

Katie helped me up, but I couldn't move my arm. It hurt like someone had hit me with a hammer. We tried to get me back on the horse, but my arm was throbbing.

"We'll walk back, and I'll lead the horses," she said.

THE END OF THE SIDEWALK

She gathered the reins of both. We walked what seemed like miles. I held my arm close to my chest and tried not to move it. Seeing the barn was a welcome sight.

Mr. Miller met us as we walked up. "What's going on? You girls look mighty hot." He saw me holding my arm. "Did you have a little upset? Let me see." He looked at my arm, shaking his head. "Young lady, I think you broke your arm. Let me get something." He took a magazine and placed it around my arm, tied it with a bandana, then took another triangle-shaped scarf and made me a sling.

"That should keep it stable," he said.

I gave him a weak smile. "Thanks. We practiced doing this in Girl Scouts, but I never thought it would happen to me."

I tried hard to not cry, but the tears ran down my face. I had ruined my perfect day. When Mom arrived, Mr. Miller went out to the car with me.

"This young lady had a little mishap," he said. "I think she broke her arm. I stabilized it, but you probably should take her to the emergency room."

"Thanks, I will," Mom said. She patted my good arm. "Don't cry, honey. We'll get you all fixed up."

We went straight to the hospital emergency room. We only waited for a few minutes until they called us back. The doctor checked my arm.

"What happened to you?" he asked.

"I fell off a horse. He stepped in a hole and reared up. It happened so fast I couldn't hold on."

"The good thing is that you have a clean break. I'm going to move your arm a little, and it may hurt, but I want to realign the bone." He started moving my arm in a gentle manner, but it still hurt. Mom grabbed my other hand and squeezed it. That helped me be a little braver. I tried not to groan, but I felt like it helped. Then he put my arm in a plaster cast and said I could use the sling I had from the stable.

"Now don't get the cast wet, and come back in four weeks. It should heal fine. No more horseback riding until you get the cast off."

I already knew that was out, but Mom nodded in agreement. I hoped she would still let me go to the rodeo. Now my dread for starting school was doubled because I'd stand out like Mary's little lamb.

Joseph patted my cast when we got home and said, "Wow, what happened? Guess I'll have to wash dishes and you'll have to dry." I told him about my accident.

"I know that hurt. Did you cry?"

"A little," I admitted.

Mom said, "She was brave. We're thankful it wasn't her left arm so she can still write and do her work at school." I liked that she told Joseph I was brave.

I wouldn't be able to ride my bike. I doubted I would be able to climb up into Miss Magnolia. I wanted to call Latrella, but I didn't have her phone number.

Dad came in, and I had to tell the story again. He gave me a big hug and said, "I'm glad you didn't get hurt worse. You look cute in a cast, I must say." Dad knew how to make me smile.

Sleeping with a cast was tricky. I tried on my back, but it was heavy lying on my stomach. I tried on my stomach with my arm up over my head, but that didn't work either. I ended up on my side resting it on the bed. My head reeled with what-ifs until I drifted off to sleep.

CHAPTER 17

I OPENED MY EYES and stared at the ceiling. A water stain in the far corner looked like its zig-zag edges were cut by a pair of pinking shears. It was a zig-zag morning for sure. Today was the day I'd been dreading for months, the first day of school at Hardy Junior High. How I'd like to go back to Poindexter with Joseph. I would feel safe in that familiar place.

I closed my eyes tight and tried to go back to sleep. I wanted to lie there, feeling the attic fan pull the cool morning breeze over me like a veil of protection. Sarah Jane had abandoned me. How would I cope without her support? Would anyone want to sit by me, or would they consider me an outcast? Would people make fun of my cast?

Dad's deep voice interrupted my thoughts. "Gertrude, are you up? Hurry and get dressed."

Poindexter, my old school, was the best. I'd always looked forward to the first day of school, but I'd never had problems like I had now. With Mom out of town, it was like she'd kind of deserted me too.

My head started hurting for real, but I forced myself out of bed and put on my white blouse and red plaid skirt. The blouse slid right over my cast. Buttoning the blouse was awkward, but I managed. I pulled on my bobby socks and slid on my penny loafers. I thought about wearing my cowboy boots, but I decided not on the first day. The cast was already going to draw attention to me. All done, I eased down the hall toward the kitchen.

Joseph finished eating his cereal and jumped up from the table. "Hey, be speedy. Dad's got to take me after he drops you off. I can't wait to see all my friends."

I ate a few bites, but I could hardly swallow. I drank some juice and went to brush my teeth.

As we got in the car, Dad said, "You look mighty pretty, gal. Let's go. You don't want to be late on your first day."

I did want to be late. If he only knew the turmoil I felt. I gulped when I saw the long tan brick building as I got out of the car. "Bye, Dad. Love you."

As he pulled off, Joseph yelled out the window, "Bye, have a great day."

I waved and started the walk toward the building, wanting to turn around and run the other way. I had imagined being with Sarah Jane, but she'd probably ridden with Polly, and I didn't see them anywhere. I headed for first period, which was English, my favorite subject. I didn't see a soul I knew, so I slid into a desk and tried to look ready.

My teacher Mrs. Bailey called the roll. A pencil stuck out of the gray bun on top of her head. She wore a pretty flowered dress, and she smiled as she said, "Class, I'd like you to write an essay about the most important thing that happened during your summer vacation."

Mulling over my options, I decided to write about Girl Scout Camp, even though Mom's appointment to the Civil Rights Commission was the most important thing. I didn't want to share that news with anyone. It would be easy to write about Camp since I loved it so much. I started writing about camping under the stars, swimming and canoeing on the lake, making s'mores, singing around the campfire, and making crafts. I got camp-sick as I reminisced. When the bell rang, I'd written two and a half pages. It was fun to lose myself in thoughts of Camp.

Coach Compton greeted everyone at the door of the science lab. I'd never had a man as a teacher before. Even the principal at Poindexter was a woman. He told us to call him Coach because he coached the tennis team. He assigned us lab partners. Thank goodness my partner was a girl. Dressed to perfection, she wore a gray straight skirt with a white blouse and a pink scarf tied around her neck. Mom said straight skirts were silly, but I knew they were popular because Polly told me she had one. Polly made sure she had the latest fashion. I looked at my plaid skirt and felt uncomfortable thinking I was out of style.

"Hi, I'm Susan," she said. "So glad you're my partner. We're going to have fun." Her brown eyes lit up with enthusiasm, and when she smiled, she had dimples on each side of her face. Her hair curved under in a perfect pageboy.

"I'm Trudy. I'm glad I didn't end up with a boy partner."

"Yeah, I know what you mean. Most guys are a pain." She wrote something on a piece of paper and handed it to me. "Here's my phone number so you can call me. Show me your schedule. Let's see if we have any other classes together. How did you break your arm?"

"I fell off a galloping horse. It doesn't hurt anymore. I'll get the cast off in a couple of weeks."

I handed her my schedule, and she smiled. "Oh good, we have chorus together." Excited by her friendliness, I worried that she might change her mind later. After class, we walked out together. A tall guy with dark-rimmed glasses came out the classroom door and passed us.

"Hi, Wes, I didn't see you in class," she said as she put her books on her hip.

"Hi, how ya doing?" He slowed to walk beside her. I started to walk ahead, but Susan grabbed my arm.

"Wait, Trudy. This is my friend Wes. We went to Whitfield together." Then she said to Wes, "Trudy's my science lab partner and my new friend."

"Hi, it's nice to meet you," I said. My cheeks got hot. "See y'all later. I gotta get to class." My nerves had gotten the best of me. I figured no guy would give me a second look.

When Susan and I met up at chorus for our last class, I smiled as I thought how Susan could help me be more confident around boys. Her friendliness made me relax a little. I loved singing, so chorus would be a fun class.

After class, we walked down the hall together.

"Where's your locker?" Susan said. "Give me your books." She grabbed them before I could say anything. The cast did make it awkward to carry them.

"It's down by my English class, number 243."

"Mine is 260, not far from yours. Where do you live?"

"955 Pecan Boulevard. It's not too far from the high school. How about you?"

"I live on First Avenue, but you're not going to believe this. My stepdad wants to buy the house at 902 Pecan Boulevard, the yellow brick one on the corner."

"Wow, that would be so cool. We could walk to school

together." She grinned and handed my books back as we reached my locker.

"See you tomorrow, Trudy. I'm glad we're lab partners."

"Me too." What a great way to end my first day.

CHAPTER 18

I STOOD BY my locker trying to figure out what to take home when Sarah Jane and Polly came up. I was relieved to see them only because I didn't want to be alone. I wished Sarah Jane and I could be together without bossy Polly.

"How'd your day go?" Sarah Jane asked. Before I could answer, Polly said, "Isn't it a lot better than Poindexter Elementary?"

"It was great. I like my classes, and I met a new girl who's my science lab partner."

"I told you," Polly said. She pushed her way in between Sarah Jane and me, then she said to Sarah Jane, "I'm excited we have three classes together. Did you notice that girl Mary Lynn? She thinks she's hot stuff, wearing that red lipstick and eye makeup. What about that cute guy in English on the front row? He smiled at me as he went out the door after class. I think his name was Justin."

She'd left me out of the conversation. As I walked home with them, I wished I had the guts to tell her to shut up and be nice. I couldn't wait to get home.

"Bye," I said, as they turned to go down Sarah Jane's street. It was like I was invisible. If I hadn't said something, they probably wouldn't even have noticed I was no longer with them.

"Oh, bye. See you tomorrow," Sarah Jane said. Polly waved and paraded on down the street. I was so mad at Sarah Jane for

THE END OF THE SIDEWALK

ignoring me that I could've spit. I ran home the rest of the way, struggling to hold my books with my cast.

The minute I opened the door, I caught whiffs of baked cookies coming from the kitchen.

"I'm home," I yelled.

"Come fill me in on your first day," Jetta Mae said.

In the kitchen, I grabbed a cookie off a plate and got the milk from the refrigerator. Jetta Mae handed me a glass. She was making her mouth-watering biscuits for our supper. She used a glass turned upside down to cut out the biscuits in perfect circles. I tried to take note of all the little things she did while she was cooking so I could do them when I started cooking.

"Let me cut them for you." I took the glass and pushed down on the dough. Then I placed the sticky circle on the cookie sheet. "My first day went okay. I met a new girl who is my science lab partner. Her name's Susan. She's cute and friendly." I didn't tell her about Polly and Sarah Jane though.

"Glad to hear it. I felt it in my bones that it would go well for you. Now I've something serious to discuss with you. What in Heaven's name were you doing in the little store by the woods at the end of the sidewalk? Cornelia said she ran into you in the store, but you left in a hurry."

"Oh, please don't tell Mom. I was trying to find Latrella. I needed to tell her something important, and Big Mama doesn't have a phone. I thought maybe I would see her, but I didn't, and I got scared. I won't do it again. I promise with a capital *P*."

"You'd better not. That store's off-limits for you. You stay on your side, you hear me?"

"I will. Girl Scout Honor." I held up the Girl Scout sign

to her. "These cookies are yummy." I grabbed a cookie and ran to change my clothes. I didn't dare say where I was headed. I wouldn't go to the store anymore, but I figured the woods were still on my side, as Jetta Mae called it.

I went to the rock to see if there was a letter from Latrella and if she had picked mine up. Sure enough, there was a letter from her. I grabbed it and headed for Miss Magnolia. I settled into my favorite place and opened her letter.

> *Dear Trudy,*
>
> *I wish we could still meet somewhere. I don't like writing letters as much. I want to be able to talk. Nobody uses these woods to walk through, except Jetta Mae and maybe a few others. Think about it. I started reading* Misty of Chincoteague. *I didn't know there was a place with wild horses. I can see why you liked it. Let's figure out a way to meet at least sometimes.*
>
> *Your friend,*
> *Latrella*

I agreed with her. Writing letters wasn't the same. I really wanted to tell her about my first day at school. I ran into the house and jotted her a quick note.

> *Dear Latrella,*
>
> *Let's meet tomorrow and talk about it. I just want us to be safe. Maybe you can come to my house with Jetta*

> Mae. I could even ask Mom about that. My first day at school went well.
>
> Your friend,
Trudy

I ran back to the woods and put my letter under the rock. I was about to leave when I heard something, and I peeked in the bushes. Latrella was smiling at me.

"What are you doing here?" I said. "I thought we were going to write letters."

"I thought I could catch you so we could talk about school. I don't want to write letters. It's boring. Whoa. What happened to your arm?"

I stepped into the bushes and sat down. I told her about falling off the horse.

"That sounds scary. You still want your own horse?"

"Of course. I don't blame the horse because he stepped in a hole. I can't wait to ride again. How about your first day? How was it?"

"Nothing special. Just like any other day." She smoothed out her blue skirt and pulled a lollipop out of her blouse pocket. She handed it to me and then pulled another one out for her.

"Thanks." The cherry lollipop tasted yummy as I rolled it around in my mouth. "I had to admit I was nervous about today. It went great. I met this new girl, and she might move to my street. We had two classes together. Nobody said anything mean." I looked around. "I better go. Somebody might hear us in here."

"So what if someone hears us? Are you ashamed of being with me?" Her dark eyes stared at me. She picked up *Misty of*

Chincoteague and shoved it in my hand. "Take your book back. I thought we were friends."

"Wait. We are friends." I grabbed her hand and gave the book back. "We must be careful. I don't want anyone to be ugly to you. We could get in trouble since we're not the same color."

"Big Mama's had white people be ugly to her before, but we're proud of who we are. I'm smart, and I'm gonna be a doctor someday. I'll show those uppity-uppity white people who think they're better than me. But right now, I know we must be careful. Did you know a sixteen-year-old Black girl got put in jail and sent to reform school because she sat down in the white waiting room and wouldn't get up?"

"No. Was that here in Jackson?"

"It was in McComb. It gets worse. Several of her friends went to the courthouse to protest, and they got expelled from school when they wouldn't leave and go home."

"That's terrible. Is the girl still at that school?" I asked.

"I guess so. I haven't heard any more about it. White folks are trying to keep it quiet."

"Jetta Mae told me about Rosa Parks getting arrested for not giving up her seat on the bus, but I didn't think they would arrest a girl. Do you think we could get arrested if they caught us?"

"No, but we can't be certain. Big Mama says we need eyes in the back of our head when it comes to being around some white people. Not you, though. Anyway, I guess it's better we don't chance it. What about meeting once every two weeks?"

"I guess we could try that." I didn't want to give up ever seeing her.

"But we're still friends, right?" She opened the book. "Can't wait to finish this book. I loved the other one. Do you have more?"

"I have plenty of books. I'd better get home now because my dad will be home soon."

"Is your dad prejudiced?"

"No, but he works all the time, so he's not involved like my mom. You'd like my dad."

"You're acting so jittery and concerned about him knowing where you are. Can't you relax and enjoy my company?" She stood up and twirled around like she didn't have a care in the world. Her bare feet stepped on the twigs and roots. She acted like she was dancing on a soft cushion.

"Doesn't that hurt your feet? I don't like to go barefooted."

"Nope. My feet are as tough as an elephant's hide. Big Mama says I was born to go shoeless. When I was little, she'd put on my shoes, and I'd take them right off. Now I wear shoes only when I'm going somewhere. Feel the bottom of my foot." She held up her foot, and when I touched it, she yelled *oowee* and laughed when I jumped.

I relaxed a little. "Who's your best friend at school?"

"I guess Tilly is my best friend. We've known each other since first grade. She's tall and thin. We sit together at lunch and sometimes spend the night together. But you're my new best friend."

"You're mine too." I felt a little guilty about Sarah Jane, but after all, she chose to spend her time with Polly and not me. I decided I could have two best friends if we ever did make up.

"Do you think your parents would mind if we called each other?" I said.

She squirmed a little. "I don't know. I haven't really told them I met you. I could tell them you go to school with me, but that would be a lie."

"I don't want you to do that. Since you came to my house with Jetta Mae, you could tell them that we met at the funeral and then we saw each other at my house. That would be true."

"Let me check, and I'll write you a letter."

"I've got to go," I said. She jumped in front of me and grabbed me in a hug.

"Thanks for the book. See you in two weeks." Then she ran out of the woods before I could answer.

CHAPTER 19

WHEN I GOT HOME, Dad pulled up alongside the curb. I waved and ran to meet him. Jetta Mae walked out the door and said goodbye. Dad went into the house, but I hung back to tell Jetta Mae my news.

"Latrella's my new best friend," I whispered to her as I passed by.

"What did you say?" She looked puzzled, so I repeated myself in a soft voice.

"That's good. All God's children should be friends." I gave her a big hug and went inside.

After supper, I practiced my piano one-handed and then started reading *King of the Wind*. The same author of *Misty of Chincoteague* wrote the book. These books made my heart ache for a horse of my own, but I still wanted to read them. At some point, I dozed off.

BOOM!

I nearly jumped out of my skin. I heard Mom and Dad's bedroom door open. The hall light came on, then Dad ran by my door. I stepped out into the hallway.

"What was that? A gunshot?" Joseph stood in the hallway rubbing his eyes. I put my arm around him and held him close.

"Stay back," Dad ordered as he peered out the window by the living room couch. He then turned on the porch light. He waited

THE END OF THE SIDEWALK

a few minutes and opened the front door enough so he could see out. He got his big flashlight and shined it all over the front yard, then went out and closed the door behind him. I prayed that no one was out there who would hurt him.

"I'm scared," said Joseph. I squeezed him even tighter.

"Me too." We huddled near the door waiting for Dad.

Dad came back inside. "Someone threw a stick of dynamite in the yard. Dad-burned teenagers I bet," he muttered. "It left a hole in the front yard. I'm going to call the police."

Joseph squirmed away from me and ran toward the door. "I want to see it."

Dad grabbed his pajama shirt and said, "Whoa, son. It's late. I don't want you going out there. I'll handle this. You two get back in bed right now. You have school tomorrow."

When I got back in bed, I started thinking of the what ifs. What if it had come through the window and caught our house on fire? What if Joseph had gotten trapped in his room and had been burned? What if someone had been waiting outside and had gotten in a fight with Dad? I put my pillow over my head to try and get away from those thoughts. I knew I needed to go back to sleep.

I heard a little knock and saw Joseph standing in the doorway. "Can I sleep in here with you?" he asked.

"Sure." I was glad he wanted to come in my room. He climbed up on the top bunk and fell asleep immediately.

As I dozed off, I found myself running through the woods, yelling for Latrella. Someone jumped out from behind a tree right in front of me. It was a policeman.

He said, "I'm arresting you." He dangled handcuffs in front of me. I froze and screamed. I screamed again and sat up in bed.

My wet pajama top clung to my body. Joseph turned over and groaned.

Dad turned on my light. "What's the matter, Princess? Are you okay?"

"I had a nightmare. It seemed so real. A policeman was arresting me."

Dad sat down on my bed and held my hand. "It was just a dream. Everything's going to be fine. Now get some sleep. It's been a rough night."

"Dad, are these things going to keep happening? I don't like it."

"I hope not. People think this is a way to upset us and make your mom stop what she's doing, but her work is important. Now go back to sleep, and we'll talk some more when your mom gets home."

He kissed my forehead and left the room, turning out the light. I snuggled down under the covers and lay there wide-eyed for what seemed like hours. I couldn't forget my dream. Would morning ever come? My heart pounded and my mouth felt as dry as the Sahara Desert.

The next morning, Joseph started asking Dad questions about the dynamite. Dad said, "I called the police and made a report. They'll ride by and check at night. Don't talk about it at school. Do you understand?"

"Yes, sir," Joseph answered, and I nodded my head. I didn't look up from my cereal because I didn't want Dad to see fear in my face. I was scared about it, plus I'd had that dream.

"Your Aunt Liz is taking you to school today," Dad said. "Be sure and be ready. I've got to get to work." Dad kissed us each on the head and left. We got our things together and sat down on the couch until Aunt Liz pulled up out front.

"Remember what Dad said," I warned Joseph. He ran out the door and pointed to the hole in the front yard as he went by it. I glanced over at it but didn't want Aunt Liz to notice. She dropped Sarah Jane and me off at the school's front entrance.

"Let's go in the end door since it's close to my locker," I told Sarah Jane. As we walked, I wanted us to talk without Polly around.

"Have you ever heard of Martin Luther King Jr.?" I said.

She shook her head. "What grade is he in?"

"He doesn't go to school here. He's a Black preacher. He's making speeches all over for equal rights for Negroes. I thought maybe you knew about him. Jetta Mae says he's wonderful and he wants to help without fighting."

As she headed upstairs to her classes, she hollered, "Never heard of him. Sorry."

She didn't even seem interested. So much for connecting with her. I decided to go to the library as soon as I could to see what more I could find out about him.

Once in English class, Mrs. Bailey walked around the room handing out our essay papers. I peeked inside the folded paper and saw an *A* in red and the comment, *Interesting topic*.

"Most of you did a good job on your first assignment," Mrs. Bailey said. "I'd like a few of you to share with the class. We had many different topics. Gertrude, will you read yours?"

I knew that I couldn't say no, but my face heated up like a hot potato. Walking to the front of the room, I prayed that I wouldn't embarrass myself by shaking. If I could lean back on the green chalkboard, I would have support, but I had to stand right in front of the desks. I got a whiff of chalk dust and worried I'd sneeze. Fearful that if I looked up I'd lose my place, I stared at the words on my paper. At first, everything blurred. I took a deep breath and started reading as fast as I could.

When I said "Girl Scout Camp," I heard a few snickers. Mrs. Bailey held up her hand, and it got quiet again. After I finished the last sentence, I breathed a sigh of relief. Still looking down, I returned to the safety of my desk. After class, I hurried to second period science lab.

When I got there, Susan tapped my cast. "Why didn't you call me?"

"Sorry. I kind of forgot. Dad said I could come over for a little while after school, though." I didn't want to tell her what had happened, not yet anyway.

After class, we walked out together. "I'll see you in chorus," she said.

In gym class, we went outside to practice tennis on the courts. Sarah Jane and I had played several times, but I'd never had lessons. Of course, I couldn't play now with my cast.

"Mrs. Johnson, would you like me to pick up the balls at the back of the court?" I said. "I have one good hand." She smiled and nodded. I didn't want to sit around while everybody else was playing.

"Have you ever played tennis?" she asked.

"Yes, ma'am. I've played with my cousin. I'd love to try out when I get my cast off. I like tennis."

"We have tryouts next week, but I'll see what I can arrange for you."

Wow. I thought being on the tennis team would be exciting. Junior high might not be bad after all. For that moment, my insides tingled.

THE END OF THE SIDEWALK

At lunch, I didn't see any familiar faces, so I got my tray and sat at a table that had some girls sitting at the other end. They looked my way, and I smiled, but they didn't invite me to sit with them. I started eating and wishing Sarah Jane or Susan would come sit beside me. Instead, I saw Polly coming toward me.

"Hi, want me to join you?" she said. She sat down before I could say anything. "Why aren't you sitting with those girls?"

"Because I don't know them, but I didn't want to eat alone. I didn't see anyone I knew until you came in."

"People will think you're stuck up if you don't talk to them, and if you tell them about your mom, they might not want to sit with you anyway."

She smiled at the girls and waved. Then she had the nerve to scoot down by them and leave me sitting alone again. She started talking to them and then they looked at me again, still not smiling. What had she told them?

Tears welled up in my eyes. Turning my head away from them, I started moving fast from the table and then my tray fell to the floor with a loud crash. I started trying to clean up the scattered mess of mashed potatoes, meatloaf, and beans, not to mention my milk that had spilled from the carton.

"Hey, let me help you."

I looked up and saw Susan's friend, the guy with the dark-rimmed glasses. I couldn't even think of his name. Embarrassed, I tried to wipe the tears from my face.

"I'm Wes, remember? I met you outside the science lab."

I nodded my head, trying to clean up the mess. Then the janitor came with a mop and motioned for me to move away. I grabbed my books and ran out of the cafeteria.

"Wait. I want to talk to you."

I knew it was Wes talking to me, but I didn't stop. I ducked into the girl's bathroom. I looked a mess. Splashing water on my face to wash away my tears, I looked in the mirror at my splotchy face. The bell rang, signaling time for the next class, but I wanted to stay in the bathroom for the rest of the day. As the splotches faded, I pinched my cheeks to make them red so it would look like I had on makeup. I wanted to go home but that wasn't an option.

Later in the afternoon, I trudged down the hall to chorus. As soon as I walked in the door, I saw Susan smiling at me. I rushed to sit down beside her. My heart pounding like a hammer in my chest, I grabbed her hand.

"What's the matter?" she asked.

"I dropped my tray in the lunchroom and made a scene. Your friend Wes tried to talk to me, but I ran out and hid in the bathroom until my next class. Every time I think about it, I get upset all over again. My cousin's friend Polly said some mean things and—"

"All right, class," said Mr. Richardson, "give me your attention. No more talking." said Mr. Richardson.

I realized I needed to tell Susan about Mom even if it meant she wouldn't be my friend.

CHAPTER 20

"LET'S LOOSEN UP our lungs and make some beautiful noise." Mr. Richardson sat at the piano, played a scale, and had us sing it. Then he started playing "America the Beautiful." He smiled as he played.

When class was over, Susan grabbed my arm. "Come on, let's get out of here."

"Dad said I could go to your house for a little while. My mom's out of town," I said.

On the way to Susan's, I explained to her what Mom was doing. I told her about the fire truck and the policeman but not the dynamite. "If you don't want me to come to your house, I understand."

"I don't care what your mom does," she said.

Boy, that was a relief to me. But then she said, "Don't say anything to my stepdad, though. He hates Colored people with a passion."

When we walked into the kitchen at her house, Susan's mom was stirring something in a pot on the stove. Susan's baby brother was sitting on the floor with her other brother and sister. I picked the baby up, jiggling him up and down. When he smiled, he had dimples just like Susan. The other two ran over and hugged Susan. They were about three and four years old. Her brother peeked out from behind her skirt and waved.

THE END OF THE SIDEWALK

"Mom, this is Trudy, my science lab partner. I'm going to show her my cheer I'm going to do for cheerleader tryouts." Mrs. Sheridan wiped her hands and took the baby.

"So nice to meet you," she said. "Betsy, Jason, pick up your toys before Trudy trips on them."

We walked down the hall to Susan's room. She threw her books on one of her twin beds covered with matching bedspreads. She pushed a chair out of the way and started doing her cheer on the spacious floor. She did a split and jumped up.

I clapped my hands. "Fantastic! I can't even do a split or jump that high." I glanced around her room, and I noticed a picture of a soldier on her bedside table.

"Who's that?" I went over and picked up the frame. The handsome man had dark eyes like Susan.

"That's my dad. He was killed in a plane crash in Korea. I was little, maybe three. I hardly remember him."

"Susan," a man's voice yelled from the kitchen, "please help your mom. Take the kids to your room." We hadn't heard her stepdad come into the house.

"I'm coming," Susan yelled back. "I happen to have company."

"Who's here? Don't you know your mother needs your help with supper and the kids?"

"Dennis, I'm coming," Susan said.

I stood behind her wanting to sneak out the door without being seen. It surprised me that she called him by his first name. Even though he wasn't her dad, my mom would have made me call him Mr. Dennis or something like that.

"Trudy and I will set the table, won't we?" she said as we walked into the kitchen. I nodded in agreement.

"Trudy, huh?" he said as he raised his bushy eyebrows. "What's your last name?" He loosened his tie, then pulled it off and tossed it on the counter. Shorter than Dad, he looked like a weightlifter.

"Scuffer, sir."

"I've heard that name before. What does your dad do?" I stiffened up, scared I might say the wrong thing.

"He's a civil engineer. He works for Ross Construction Company." I shifted from one foot to the other, squeezing my hands behind my back.

"Well, you'd better run along home. Susan has chores to do." He walked toward the door.

"Wait," Susan said. "Let her stay and help. I wanted to finish showing her my cheer."

"Help your mother with these kids. Get them out of the kitchen. Now."

Susan grabbed Betsy's and Jason's hands.

"You can show her your cheer another time," he said.

"See you tomorrow," I said as I started out the door. The baby waved his hand and said bye-bye three or four times. I waved back. Then I remembered I'd left my books in Susan's room. "Let me get my stuff. We came straight from school."

"Be quick about it," he said, frowning. I was glad he hadn't asked about my mom.

Once home, I gathered some leaves to cover up the blackened hole in the yard. Though Dad told Mom about it on the phone, I didn't want it staring at her like the yard had a black eye. As I reached the top step, I looked over and saw a big crack in the window to Mom's office. It gave me the shivers. I didn't know if Dad knew about it or not.

Later during the drive to pick up Mom at the airport, Joseph talked the whole fifteen minutes. I snuggled down on the soft leather seat covers of Dad's Mercury and searched the darkening sky for the airplane.

"I see lights in the sky over there," I said and pointed. "Look. Is that her airplane?"

"I imagine that's her plane," Dad replied. "This airport isn't that busy."

"It's getting closer," Joseph yelled. "It's getting ready to land." He bounced up and down on the seat.

Once inside the airport, we went out the back door and stood behind the fence that surrounded the building. Soon the plane taxied down the runway and pulled up to the gate. Men ran out and gave directions, waving flashlights in the air like sparklers on the Fourth of July. The propellers spun fast, then slowed to a stop. The metal door opened, and two men rolled some steel steps up to the doorway. People started coming down the stairs. Then we saw Mom. Dad grabbed Joseph's shirt collar to keep him from running out onto the runway.

As soon as Mom came through the gate, Joseph almost knocked her down with an enthusiastic hug She and Dad embraced. He kept his arm around her shoulder as she and I hugged. She squeezed my hand. "I missed you, Mom," I murmured. We went to the baggage area to get her suitcase.

"I missed you too. I want to hear everything about school." She pulled me to her in a hug.

A policeman walked by and stood by the door, staring at us. Dad smiled as we went out, nodding his head, but the policeman looked the other way. Then two police cars followed us to Pecan

Boulevard. They kept going straight when we turned.

"Hey, Mom" Joseph said, "somebody threw dynamite in our yard, and there's a big hole. Wait till you see it."

"Your mom knows, son. I told her on the phone," Dad said. He turned to her. "I did call the police after we talked. They came out and filed a report. I noticed a crack in the window of your office too. I requested extra surveillance, but I doubt they'll do it."

As soon as we got home, Joseph jumped out of the car, went over to the pile of leaves I'd gathered, and started pushing them away. "See, Mom, right here. See this big hole. Look at the black mark on the steps. It was louder than a firecracker." Joseph was so excited about it. I just wanted to forget it happened.

"Stop," I yelled, because it made me think of my nightmare.

Mom walked over to the exposed hole, leaned down, and picked up some of the charred dirt and burnt grass in her hand. She studied it and then let the dirt slide out of her fingers back onto the ground. She shook her head. "I can't understand some people. Full of hate." I slipped my hand into hers. Dad stepped in and took her arm.

"Come on, Honey. Let's go in the house," Dad said.

Joseph hopped up the steps and said, "Can you believe it, Mom? You should have heard how loud it was." He yelled *BOOM!* as loud as he could.

"It scared me so much I had a nightmare," I said. "I hate the people who keep bothering us."

"Now, Gertrude," Mom said, "let's not use the word hate. There's enough of that in the world. I know you're upset, and I am too. I didn't expect this."

While Mom was unpacking, I started practicing piano. I

THE END OF THE SIDEWALK

could play with my left hand but always had a hard time playing with both hands together. I had to look at my hands, and it slowed me down. My cast gave me an excuse to play with one hand. I stopped and went to Mom and Dad's bedroom.

"Mom, could I talk to you?" She sat at her desk in her little office. I wanted to ask her about going to the rodeo with Katie. Dad sat at his desk in their bedroom. She looked up at me and then glanced at the mail.

"Gertrude, can we talk about it later? I need to go through this mail."

"Yes, ma'am," I said, but I wanted to say it would only take a minute.

Irritated that I couldn't talk to her, I tried to consider that she'd just gotten home and had a lot on her mind. I knew it was self-centered of me to be upset.

After finishing my homework and reading awhile, I got ready for bed. As I lay in bed, the attic fan's loud hum pulled the night breeze through my window, and I thought about how to be brave like Latrella had said. I was almost asleep when Mom walked into my room. She sat down on my bed.

"Gertrude, I'm sorry I was short with you earlier. I have a big meeting with the commission tomorrow, and I needed to go through all that mail. What did you want to talk about?"

Thrilled to have a few minutes of one-on-one time with her, I shared some school news first. "My gym teacher said I could try out for the tennis team when I got my cast off. Is it okay for me to try out?"

"Yes, I think that would be fine. You've always been athletic." Somehow, I never knew that Mom thought I was athletic.

"Is that what you wanted talk with me about?" she said.

I couldn't believe Mom was sitting on my bed, giving me her full attention, so I'd better not pass up the opportunity. I took a deep breath and sighed.

"What is it?" she asked.

"Are you nervous about the dynamite? You didn't say much about it. I don't like all these things happening at night. It makes it hard to go to sleep, and I can't help but be scared."

"I'm quite upset about it, but it's not going to stop me from doing what I think is right. If I stop because of that, then things won't ever change. It's a matter of standing up for what I believe in. When I went to that church meeting last year in Philadelphia, there were white women and Black women all sitting together and praying. I thought that is the way it should be everywhere. When I came back, I met Mrs. Clarie Harvey. You met her at the prayer meeting. She shared my feelings about integrating our prayer groups. She and I have become good friends. She's helping with voter registration, and her organization Womanpower Unlimited is a strong force in the Negro community. Try not to worry. Your dad talked to the police, and they're going to do a drive-by each night. I can't guarantee we won't have some more interruptions, but I hope not."

"Okay, I'll try. There's one more thing I wanted to ask you. Katie asked me to go to the rodeo with her on Saturday. I want to go, but I'd miss our first Girl Scout meeting. Is it okay if I miss one meeting? Please let me go."

She smiled at me. "Honey, I think it will be fine for you to go. I may have to change the Girl Scout meeting date anyway, but it won't hurt for you to miss one time."

"Oh my gosh. Thanks, Mom." I grabbed her hand and

squeezed it.

"Is there anything else?" I shook my head no, and she continued, "Dr. Beittel invited me to a play at Tougaloo next week. Your dad has a vestry meeting at the church and can't go. Would you like to go with me? I think it would be educational for you."

"Yes, ma'am, I'd like to go."

She stood up to leave, and I jumped up and gave her a big hug. I had some reservations about going to Tougaloo, the Negro college, but since she'd said I could go the rodeo with Katie, I didn't want to say no.

"Thanks, Mom. I love you." After she left, the scent of her perfume lingered on my hands. I snuggled down under the sheets, smiling to myself and holding my hands up to my face to breathe in the aroma of the special moment.

CHAPTER 21

THE NEXT DAY Mom took Sarah Jane and me to school. Sarah Jane chatted, acting like things were back to normal with us. Maybe it was because Polly wasn't around, but I'd take it.

"I have tennis tryouts this afternoon," I said after we walked into the school.

"How are you going to try out with that cast on your arm?" she said.

"Mrs. Johnson said for me to go, and when I get my cast off, Coach will let me try out. I told her you and I had played."

"Did you tell her you beat me hands down?" She laughed as she went up the stairs. I didn't tell her that I was going by the library to find information on Martin Luther King Jr. or that I wanted to know more about him.

When I approached the desk, the librarian smiled. "Hi, I'm Mrs. Harris. What can I do for you, young lady?"

"I wanted to find some information on Martin Luther King Jr."

"Now why do you want to read about him?" she asked, her smile turning to a frown.

"Why not? Jetta Mae says he's famous, and I want to know more about his work."

"I'm sorry, we don't have anything here in our library that I know of. I'll check and see. Is there anything else? You'd better get to class." She turned quickly, picking up some books to put on the shelves. When I stood there staring at her, she spoke again. "Go on now. You don't want to be late to class."

It irked me that she wouldn't help me find any material about him.

After chorus, Susan and I rushed to the gym to change for tennis tryouts. I changed so I could collect the balls like I did before. I would be thrilled when I got my cast off.

"Have you ever heard of Martin Luther King Jr.?" I asked.

"No, does he go to school here?" Susan stuffed her clothes into her locker.

"He's a Negro preacher for civil rights. He's supposed to be famous."

"Never heard of him. Tell me later. We'd better hurry and get on the court." Susan didn't show much interest, either. Maybe Latrella could help me find out more details.

Once outside, the girls were on one court and the boys on another. I looked over at the boys and felt conspicuous with my cast. They probably wondered what I was doing there.

"Come on, Trudy," Susan said. "What are you thinking about?"

"Thinking about being brave," I said.

She gave me a questioning look. "Come on, silly."

Those trying out started running, and then Coach put them through all sorts of drills. He paired them up, and they played doubles as he looked on. He watched them serve and had them volley the ball back and forth. I stood at the back and tossed the balls back to the girls. I steered clear of the boys' courts.

"Good work, girls and boys," Coach said. "I'll post the results tomorrow on the board in the gym. You all did a good job.

"Trudy, thanks for being our ball retriever."

"Sure," I said and smiled. "I get my cast off in ten days."

As everyone started to leave, I said to Susan, "Whew, that was quite a workout. You played great."

"Thanks, I love tennis," she said.

"*Oowee*, if it isn't one-armed Trudy," a high-pitched voice jeered at me. I turned around, and it was one of the girls from the lunchroom. She whispered something to the girl beside her, and they laughed.

"Who's that?" Susan asked.

"The girls Polly joined when I dropped my tray. I think she told them about my mom."

"Don't be a doofus," she said to me then hollered to the girls, "Get lost." She grabbed my hand, and we ran by them into the girls' locker room.

"That aggravates me to the nth degree," I said. "Please walk home with me. I don't want to walk by myself."

"Don't let those girls get under your skin. Of course, I'll walk with you. It's only a block away from my house."

"I know I shouldn't let them bother me, but I'm not brave like my mom."

As we reached my street, I saw Jetta Mae walking on the other side.

"Come on, there's Jetta Mae on her way to the bus stop. She's going to visit her sister. I want you to meet her." We ran across the street right by the azalea bushes and caught up with her.

"Jetta Mae, this is Susan, my new friend." Susan shook hands with her.

"Why, aren't you a pretty gal?" Jetta Mae said. "Nice to meet you."

THE END OF THE SIDEWALK

"Can we walk with you? Susan lives near the bus stop."

At the corner, a young man leaned against the bus stop sign. He wore a nice pair of black slacks with a white shirt and tie. He stared at us. The bus pulled up. When the doors opened, he stepped right in front of Jetta Mae. Then he turned around and laughed in her face. She put her money in and then went to the back door and got on. I wanted Jetta Mae to be like Rosa Parks.

"Are you getting on the bus, young lady?" the driver asked me.

"No, sir, but did you see what happened? That man, he—"

"Back away from the door," he said, ignoring my question. I stepped back by Susan as the door closed.

"It's ridiculous that Jetta Mae had to sit in the back of the bus when there were all those seats in the front," I said. "She couldn't even walk down the aisle. She had to use the back door. I'm going to tell Mom right now. That dumb bus driver didn't do anything."

"He might lose his job if he gets involved," Susan said. "I know it isn't right, but he knows saying something won't do any good. My stepdad says we would all get along great if the Colored people just stayed separate. We would leave them alone if they left us alone."

"Is that what you think?" I asked.

"I haven't given it much thought to tell the truth, but I didn't like the way Jetta Mae was treated."

"In Montgomery, Alabama, a Negro woman named Rosa Parks sat at the front of the bus and wouldn't give up her seat to a white person, so she got arrested. The Negro people in the city decided to not ride buses until they could sit where they wanted to. Dr. Martin Luther King Jr. helped them, and they didn't ride the buses for over a year. Finally, the Whites said the Negroes could sit where they wanted, and I think it should be that way here too."

"How do you know about that?" she asked.

"Jetta Mae told me. She knows about a lot of things that need to change to be fair to the Negroes."

When I got home, I heard the piano playing. Mom was teaching a lesson. She put her finger to her lips indicating no interruptions. Couldn't she tell I was upset?

"I need to tell you something important," I whispered. The girl stopped playing and looked at me then Mom.

"Isabel, practice this piece one more time. I'll be right back." Mom followed me into the kitchen.

"What happened?" she asked.

"Some white man stepped right in front of Jetta Mae when she was trying to pay on the bus. He laughed at her when she put her money in and then went to the back door to get on. He was so rude. The bus driver didn't do anything or say a word. He asked us if we were getting on the bus. When I said no, he told us to move out of the way and closed the door and left. It was terrible the way that man acted. There weren't that many people on the bus, but she still had to use the back door and sit in the back. That doesn't make sense to me." I talked fast and furious, but Mom stopped me.

"I need to get back to Isabel, but I agree with you. That was rude and unfair. We can talk some more later. I'm glad you told me. I'll talk to Jetta Mae about it." Mom went back to finish her piano lesson.

I called Sarah Jane. Her cheeriness that morning gave me hope that we could get back to being best friends.

THE END OF THE SIDEWALK

"Can you meet me at Miss Magnolia? I have something to tell you."

She hesitated and then said, "Only for a few minutes. I've got a lot of homework."

"Okay, I'll beat you there." I hung up the phone, raced out to Miss Magnolia, and when Sarah Jane arrived, I acted like I'd been there awhile by leaning back on a branch.

She laughed. "Okay, so I had farther to come. What's up?"

I told her what happened at the bus stop.

"That's awful," she said. "Poor Jetta Mae. Was she mad?"

"I think so, but she didn't say anything. That man was mean. Things like that happen to Negroes all the time. Latrella said that white people had been mean to her grandmother."

Sarah Jane stared at me. "What? Latrella? Who's that?"

"Her grandmother is related to Jetta Mae. I met her at the funeral. She's funny and smart. Sometimes we meet in the woods and talk. I let her borrow some of my books. You'd like her."

"I can't believe you're meeting with her. You know white and Black children aren't allowed to mix. That's as dangerous as going to see the Freedom Riders."

"No, it's not. No one can see us. We have a good hiding place, and no one comes through there anyway. She stays with her grandmother after school because her dad's a professor at Jackson State, and her mother works there too."

"You better stop meeting her. You're going to end up in trouble again. Do your mom and dad know?"

"No, but once Latrella came to work with Jetta Mae because her grandmother had an appointment. Mom met her then. We want to see if she can come again. We had a good time."

"Look, I've gotta go. You're acting a little crazy."

"I am not. You hang around with Polly all the time, and I know she doesn't like me. You can tell her the feeling is mutual. She's a smarty-pants. I can't ever do anything with you anymore. You like her better than you do me. You're starting to act just like her."

Sarah Jane frowned and said, "I don't like her better, but I don't like the way you're acting. You're wrong about Polly too. You're just jealous. I don't know what has gotten into you, but I'm leaving. You're making a big mistake. When you get in trouble, don't say I didn't warn you." She jumped down from the tree and ran over to her house without looking back.

Heck, I shouldn't have said anything about Latrella. Sarah Jane had better not tell her mom. I really thought she would want to meet Latrella. I wanted us to have our special bond again, but she'd left in a huff. I started crying. I didn't want to lose my best friend, but it seemed I already had.

CHAPTER 22

THE NEXT DAY after school, Mom met me at the door with a letter in her hand. She looked upset.

"Do you know who this is from?" she asked.

"No, ma'am. Who?" I didn't like her tone of voice.

"It's from the mayor of Itta Bena. He says you wrote him a letter. Did you say he was rude?"

"Well, I did say that because he said you were subversive. I looked up that word, and I know you aren't. He said I wouldn't be proud of you, but I said I was. Why would he say things like that?"

Mom sat down and I sat down beside her.

"Have you been reading my mail?" she said. "How did you see the letter from him?"

"I was putting some clothes away, and it was open on your desk. I looked at it, and I decided to read it. What he said made me mad, so I wrote him back. Why would someone who is a mayor write such an ugly letter?"

Mom answered, "Listen, I know you were trying to help, but next time, you need to talk to me about it first. I'll let you read some of the letters if you like. I have some very nice ones, and then I have some like his. People who are against integration have strong feelings about it. The mayor thinks I had you write the

THE END OF THE SIDEWALK

letter, and he said I was wrong to involve my children. I want you to understand how I feel. I want you to see me standing up for what I believe is right. I'm not going to bother writing him back because his mind is set, and I can't change it. I'll try to answer any questions you may have, but don't do something like this again without checking with me first."

"I'm sorry, I'm sorry. I should have talked to you about it first. I will from now on."

When Thursday arrived, I got the jitters after school thinking about the play. Mom had invited her friend Mrs. Clarie Harvey to go with us. I looked forward to talking to her but was nervous that another policeman might stop us. It had rained earlier, so it had cooled off outside. I put on my favorite brown dress with a big white collar. I glanced in the mirror to make sure my slip didn't show, then went to meet Mom.

Mom's wide-brimmed hat fluttered in the breeze. She wore a blue dress that matched her eyes. Joseph was over at Aunt Liz's to play with Frank, and Dad would pick him up after his meeting. Mrs. Harvey arrived, and we all sat in the front seat of our car with me in the middle. I'd brought *King of the Wind* with me in case I wanted to read on the way.

Mrs. Harvey saw my book and said, "You must like to read. Did you know that my mom was the first Negro librarian in the state of Mississippi? She saw to it that I had a book to read all the time."

"I love to read, especially about horses. I want one of my own one day. I'm going to a rodeo with my friend Katie. She has her own horse. I went riding with her and fell off the horse. That's how I got this broken arm. I'm getting my cast off tomorrow." I wanted to turn around and check to see if any police were following us, but I was so squished between her and Mom that I couldn't look behind me.

"Do you know of Dr. Martin Luther King Jr.?" I asked.

She smiled and nodded. "I got to hear him preach in Atlanta. He has a powerful message for us. He led the people when they boycotted the buses in Montgomery. The Black people there did a lot of walking that year, but they were able to sit wherever they wanted on the buses after that."

"Jetta Mae told me about him and Rosa Parks. He needs to do that here," I said. "Jetta Mae should be able to sit wherever she wants on the bus, I think."

"I think so too. The Freedom Riders have helped us to see that changes need to happen."

We rode by the airport and the city golf course. We passed by Lilly Street where Jetta Mae's sister lived. I recalled when Mom got stopped by the police after dropping Jetta Mae off that day. Stirring up my jitters wouldn't help, so I tried to think about horses.

Mom and Mrs. Harvey chatted as the road out to the college went for miles. I gazed out the window at the pink clouds. They looked like cotton candy. I thought about eating cotton candy at the fair and it sticking to my fingers and melting in my mouth. I saw some thin clouds stretching across the sky like party streamer decorations. Treetops lined the edge of the horizon as the sun slipped out of sight. It was a beautiful sunset. I thought about the sunsets at Girl Scout Camp by the lake.

"I love this time of day," I said. "It reminds me of Camp."

"Me too," Mom said with a smile.

"Remember that song 'Do Lord?'"

"Yes, I do." She started singing it, and I sang along with her. Mrs. Harvey joined in. I could picture Mom singing the song when she had gone to Girl Scout Camp. She would have jumped up and clapped her hands and then waved them in the air. When we finished singing, we all laughed. It felt good to share a laugh.

"Did you know that song is called a spiritual?" Mrs. Harvey asked me. "The slaves used to sing it when they were working in the fields."

"No, but I love it. It's one of my favorites."

We passed a black car sitting on the side of the road with a couple of teenage white boys sitting on the hood and holding a sign that said WE HATE FREEDOM RIDERS. Mom didn't say anything. One threw an egg, and it splattered on the window. Thank goodness the window was rolled up, or the egg would have hit Mrs. Harvey in the face. The boys yelled some ugly words.

"Did you see that sign?" I said. "Why are they out here?"

"Some Freedom Riders have come by car and are staying at Tougaloo," Mom said. "Like your dad says, those teenagers have nothing better to do with their time."

"I thought all the Freedom Riders were in jail or at Parchman." I squirmed in my seat.

"The majority did come by bus, but the ones here are helping with voter registration."

At the next curve, I saw the entrance to Tougaloo. A white wrought iron arch stretched across the road. It said *Tougaloo College 1871*. A huge white mansion stood inside the gates.

"That's Tougaloo Mansion," Mom said. "It's the oldest building on campus."

"Who lives there?" I asked as I peered out the window.

"It was the plantation home of John Boddie, but now it's used for receptions and meetings. It was bought from Boddie to be used as a school for freed slaves."

"I'd like to live in a big house like that. I could even have a horse in the backyard. Maybe Jetta Mae could live with us?"

"You have some big ideas, don't you?" Mom patted my leg and smiled.

We pulled into the parking lot. Many Black people walked toward the auditorium. The women had on hats and nice dresses like Mom. Most of the men wore suits, and I wondered why people dressed up to come to see a play. Some students walked by. One was wearing a shirt with Tougaloo written across the front. A few of the students were white.

"Are those some of the Freedom Riders?" I said as we walked toward the auditorium.

"Yes, I believe so," Mom said.

They looked about the age of Caroline and Justine who had come to the house. I was glad to see a few more white people, although I didn't see anyone my age. Several people spoke to Mom as we found a seat near the middle of the auditorium. I sat between Mom and Mrs. Harvey.

The lights dimmed, and Dr. Beittel walked out on the stage. He reminded everyone that *Raisin in the Sun* was a Broadway hit. "Our Tougaloo theatrical group has worked hard on the play, and we hope you will enjoy it."

At intermission, Dr. Beittel went back on the stage. "I want to recognize some people in the audience. Mrs. Clarie Harvey the Director of Womanpower Unlimited, Mrs. June Scuffer the Chairman of the Civil Rights Advisory Committee, Mr. Medgar

Evers the Field Secretary for the NAACP, and Rabbi Perry Nussbaum—will you all please stand? We thank you for the work you're doing in bringing justice to all people." They stood up.

When everybody clapped, I felt proud and happy. Soon the lights dimmed again, and I hoped the second half went fast. Trying hard to concentrate on the play, my mind drifted to thoughts of the long ride home in the dark.

The sound of clapping and cheering filled the auditorium as the play ended. People gave the performers a standing ovation. I clapped to join with the others. All the actors took several bows.

After the play, we didn't leave right away because Mom and Mrs. Harvey spoke to many people. Dr. Beittel came over to us and took my hand.

"Did you enjoy the play?" he asked. "Come on, I want you to meet my wife."

"Yes, sir," I said as we walked into a reception hall where Mrs. Beittel was serving punch.

"Shirley, this is Gertrude Scuffer, June's daughter. I thought she might help you serve."

"Why certainly," she said. "How pretty you look tonight. I'm glad you came with your mother. I've enjoyed getting to know her."

"Thank you," I said and smiled as she handed me the ladle. I filled the cups and kept smiling as people gathered in the room for refreshments. I was glad I had something to do. The crowd thinned out soon since the play was long and it was getting late.

"We'd better head for home," Mom said as I handed Mrs. Harvey and her each a cup of punch.

"Your daughter was so nice to serve," Mrs. Beittel said. "Bring her back anytime."

"I'm sure she was happy to help," Mom replied. "It was lovely."

As we left the parking lot, almost all the other cars were already gone. The dark road looked spooky as we left the campus. The sliver of a moon and the stars offered little light. The lights of the campus seemed far away as we rode into the shadowy darkness.

I saw that same black car on the side of the road right outside the gate. As we passed by, they turned on their lights and pulled out right behind us. A teenage boy leaned out the window and yelled, "Quit hogging the road."

The car got right on our bumper. The headlights flashed on bright. Mom sped up. The car sped up too. It pulled up alongside us. They rolled down the window and started throwing eggs.

Splat, splat, splat.

"Don't look at them," Mom said. I wanted to crawl on the floor of the car, but I sat as close as I could to Mom, and I grabbed Mrs. Harvey's hand. My heart pounded in my chest so hard it hurt. Mom went faster, but they continued to ride beside us on the wrong side of the road. They were laughing and yelling. I was scared out of my skin. Their words blurred together so it sounded like a roar.

"Our Father, who art in Heaven . . ." I prayed out loud. Mom kept her eyes on the road. Where were the police when we needed them? I wanted someone to appear and help us.

Mom looked in the rear-view mirror. "I see some headlights back behind us."

The car sped away. Mom slowed down but was still silent.

Mrs. Harvey broke the silence and said, "June, you handled that very well. I'm afraid we must deal with that kind of foolishness all the time now when we go out at night. I've never had my

THE END OF THE SIDEWALK

car egged before, but many times they ride close and shine their bright lights."

"I'm glad you came with us, Clarie," Mom said. "I'm sorry we encountered those protesters. I'm thankful they didn't make us run off the road. I'm trembling all over."

"I am too. I enjoyed the play so much, but this situation was frightening."

I didn't see any car lights behind us. That car Mom saw must have turned off. Once again, we were all alone on the dark road. Breathing hard, I saw a stoplight, a sign that we were back in civilization again. Mom seemed to relax, but I was scared to even utter a sound. I felt safe, sitting between them, glad that we had made it off that long dark road. I could see the remains of the egg on the car windows.

"Do some white students go to Tougaloo?" I said. "I thought that I saw some."

"Yes, some do," Mom said.

"How come white students can go there, but Negro students can't go to our schools?"

"Most places in the South still promote the Separate but Equal slogan, but the problem is that things are not equal."

"Last year a little Negro girl named Ruby Bridges went to an all-white school in New Orleans," Mrs. Harvey said. "She was only six years old. The US Marshalls had to escort her to protect her. Then nobody else would go to school. She kept going, though."

"I believe the day is coming when all schools here will be integrated," Mom said. "We're working toward that now." I noticed Mom's hand shaking a little.

"Are you scared, Mom?"

"Not now, but that encounter with those teenagers did shake me up. I've never had anything like that happen before."

"It scared me for sure. I'm glad I was stuck between the two of you."

When we arrived home, Mom and Mrs. Harvey hugged and then Mrs. Harvey gave me a hug too. "I'm glad you went with us. June, I enjoyed the play." She got in her car and drove off.

"Are you going to tell Dad what happened to us?" I asked.

"Certainly. I know he'll be upset, but I'm still going to tell him." Mom put her arm around me, and we walked into the house together.

Tiptoeing into the kitchen, I got a drink of water because my mouth felt like I'd eaten a pack of crackers in one bite. The cool water soothed my throat. The clock over the refrigerator said ten-thirty. Creeping down the hall and into my bedroom, I found my pajamas hanging on a hook in my closet.

Slipping into my pajamas, I climbed into bed. I closed my eyes, but my mind saw those guys yelling and screaming at us, my ears heard the eggs hitting the windows, and my heart skipped a beat. I thought about Mom, how she'd handled herself by driving fast but not yelling back or reacting to what they said. I didn't know if I could have kept my composure had I been the one driving. Even though I was safe at home, I shivered under the sheets.

CHAPTER 23

AT SCHOOL the next day, I saw Sarah Jane and Polly going up the steps. Polly looked my way and said in a sassy sort of way, "Hey, Trudy."

I wanted to imitate her, but when Sarah Jane looked my way, I chickened out. I didn't want to make matters worse with us, so I said, "Hey, Polly. Hey Sarah Jane. See ya later."

Determined to not think about my last meeting with Sarah Jane, I settled my mind with the thought that my arm would be cast-free this afternoon. Yay! And this coming Saturday, I would be going to the rodeo with Katie. Even though I wouldn't be riding, I would be surrounded by horses. I decided to go see Whisper after my doctor appointment. I hadn't been by there in a while.

"Hey, Trudy." I turned and beside me stood Wes, the guy with the glasses who had helped me in the lunchroom.

"Hi, how are you?" I said as I slowed down a bit.

"Fine. How's your arm doing?"

I noticed his dark hair, combed nicely in place. I looked straight at him and tried to act calm. "Oh, I think it's all healed. I'm getting my cast off today. Hey, listen, sorry about running out of the lunchroom the other day. I was upset." I shifted my books in my arms.

THE END OF THE SIDEWALK

"Sure. Say, did you know that my mom knows your mom from being in Church Women United? She said your mom was a good president."

"What church do you go to?" I asked.

"Grace Methodist. How about you?"

"St. Columb's Episcopal. It's up there on Claiborne."

"Ours is on West Capitol. It's not far from yours," he said.

We reached my classroom too soon. I wanted to tell him about going to the rodeo.

"Well, bye, I'll see you later," he said and moved on down the hall.

I thought he was nice, and talking to him wasn't hard once we started.

During second period science lab, I wanted to tell Susan about what happened at Tougaloo, but I didn't want anyone else to hear. I decided to wait.

"Guess what?" she said. "I made the tennis team. I know you'll make it when you try out."

"That's great. I knew you would. If I make it, maybe we can be partners."

"You bet," she laughed and squeezed my arm.

"You're going to be busy with tennis and cheerleading."

I glanced over at Wes, and my heart skipped a beat. Did I have a crush on him? We smiled at each other. Coach started our lesson, so the moment passed. After class, I was walking down the hall when two girls passed by. One of them knocked my arm, and my books fell to the floor.

"Oh, excuse me," she said as she kept moving.

When I scrambled to pick up my books, a couple of people

stopped and bent down to help. I mumbled thanks and tried to brush it off. Dumb girls.

After school, Mom and I drove to the doctor to get my cast off.

"Do you think Latrella and I could be friends like you and Mrs. Harvey?" I asked.

"What do you mean?" Mom glanced my way, then looked straight ahead.

"She could come over to my house again, and we could talk on the phone sometimes."

"I doubt her parents would allow it. It might feel risky to them. It was different when you weren't in school and she came with Jetta Mae. Now there's little time in the afternoon before Jetta Mae goes home. You could talk on the phone. I don't object to that, but she would need permission from her parents."

"Do you know her parents? They both work at Jackson State. Her dad is a math professor."

"No, I don't know them. I could ask Jetta Mae to give me their number, and I could call."

"Would you? Oh, that would be great." I squirmed in my seat with excitement.

"Don't jump to conclusions. Her parents may not be in favor of it. We must be careful of their feelings because such friendships aren't the custom."

"I wish things were different. I like Latrella."

"Maybe someday they will be. I hope so."

Even though I hadn't told Mom about meeting Latrella, at least I had talked to her about us being friends.

"This guy at school in my science lab said his mother was in Church Women United with you. She said you were a good president."

"What's her name?" she asked. I realized I didn't even remember Wes's last name.

"I don't know, but I'll find out."

We arrived at the doctor's office. I couldn't wait to get the cast removed. The doctor said my arm had healed and took off the cast.

"Young lady, don't go falling off any more horses," he said.

"Don't worry. I'm going to be extra careful."

On the way home, I talked to Mom about the night of the play. "What did Dad say when you told him what happened on our way home?"

"He was upset, but I expected that. He doesn't want me going to any night activities like that unless he can go. He washed the car down before he went to work."

"Do you think those guys were members of the Ku Klux Klan?"

"No, the Ku Klux Klan is made up of men who dress in white robes and hoods so no one can tell who they are. They've done some terrible things to Negroes, like burning the Freedom Rider bus and burning churches. Where did you hear about them?"

"Somebody said they dressed up like ghosts and scared Negro people. Those guys scared me so much I wondered if they were like them. Do you know anyone who's a member?"

"No, but the White Citizens Council is trying to stop any form of integration. That's why they arrest the Freedom Riders. Many white people in Jackson think that way. It's unfair, in my opinion." She stopped the car at our house.

I jumped out and threw my arms in the air, shouting, "Hot diggedy dog. I got my cast off."

I ran in the house. My arm felt light as a cotton ball compared to when I had the cast on it. I started to call Sarah Jane, but then I remembered she was mad at me. I guessed I should apologize for what I'd said about her acting like Polly, but it was the truth.

"Where's Joseph?" I asked as I ran into the kitchen.

"I think he went over to Frank's," Jetta Mae said, "if he's not out back."

"Look, my cast is gone. Yippee!" I waved my arm up and down.

She gave me a hug and laughed. "We need to celebrate. How about some cookies and milk?" We sat together and chatted while I ate three cookies.

"How's school?" she asked.

"It's good, except for some prissy girls. I try to ignore them. Susan made the tennis team, and now I can try out next week because I have my cast off. Tomorrow I'm going to the rodeo with Katie. I think it will be the best day of my life."

"I hope so. You can tell me all about it next week."

"Did you know that Mrs. Harvey's mom was the first Negro librarian in the whole state and that Mrs. Harvey runs a funeral home for Negroes?"

"I didn't know about her mom, but we used her funeral home when my mom died. They really treated us kindly. I'd better be going," she said.

"I'll walk with you," I said, and we headed to the end of the sidewalk. I hoped just maybe Latrella would be there. She sometimes hid in the woods even when I didn't come.

THE END OF THE SIDEWALK

After I was sure Jetta Mae was out of hearing distance, I murmured, "Latrella, are you here?" I went into the woods and looked under the rock to see if there was a letter, but there wasn't. I didn't see her in our regular place, so I started to leave. She jumped out from behind a tree and said *boo*.

I almost lost my balance when I stepped back. "Girl, you scared me so much, I nearly wet my pants."

"Where have you been? I came after two days, and you never showed up."

"We said two weeks, not two days. I have a good excuse. I went somewhere with my mom and her friend. I got my cast off today. You didn't even notice."

"Give me a chance." She rubbed my arm, and we sat down together. I told her about what happened at Tougaloo.

"I was thankful to be seated between Mom and Mrs. Harvey," I said. "I felt safer than if I had been sitting by myself. I scrunched down in the seat as far as I could. It was real scary."

"I'm glad you're okay," she said. "Was your mom scared, too?"

"Yes, we all were, but Mom kept driving and looking straight ahead. She was brave."

"My dad has had white people follow too close behind his car and flash their bright lights," Latrella said. "He doesn't drive at night unless it is important."

"Did you ask if I could call you? I talked to Mom about you coming over again, but she said now that we're in school, it would be too late because Jetta Mae leaves at four-thirty."

"No, but give me your phone number, and I'll call you. Did you tell your mom we were meeting?"

"No. I didn't want to chance her saying we couldn't. Here's

my phone number." I didn't have any paper, so I wrote it in the dirt with a stick, 353-6756. She jumped up and started singing three-five-three-dash-six-seven-five-six, over and over. Then she shouted, "I know it." She covered her eyes and sang it again. I laughed and started singing with her.

She stopped and said, "Did you know that last year four Black students went into a Woolworth's and sat down at the lunch counter? The cooks wouldn't serve them lunch, so they just sat there all day until the store closed. The police came but couldn't arrest them because they weren't doing anything but sitting. The next day more students came and then more and more. Finally, Woolworth's had to change their policy and serve them because no white people would even come, and the store wasn't doing any business. My dad told me about it."

"I bet if they did that here," I said, "they would get arrested just like the Freedom Riders. I wish we could be friends out in the open. Why should anyone care what we do? We aren't bothering anyone."

Latrella picked a leaf off the bush and broke it into little pieces. "I know, but we're not the same color," she said, frowning. "Some people don't think we should be friends. What do you think?"

"We talked about this last time. You yourself said we needed to be careful. Give me your phone number, and my mom will call your mom."

"It's 352-4001."

I repeated it to myself a few times. I wanted to be friends with her, but I didn't want either of us to get in trouble. Mom didn't worry so much about getting in trouble. She did what she felt was the right thing even when people criticized and despised her.

THE END OF THE SIDEWALK

"I want us to be friends." I meant what I said with all my heart. I didn't care what Sarah Jane said anymore.

Latrella grabbed my hand. "That settles it. We're friends, no matter what." I liked her determination about what she believed.

As I left the woods, she was singing three-five-three-dash-six-seven-five-six. I smiled and skipped all the way down the sidewalk to home.

CHAPTER 24

TODAY WAS Rodeo Day. We drove over to Katie's, and I was wearing jeans and my cowboy boots. I wished I had a real cowboy hat because I wanted to look like I belonged even if I wasn't riding.

Katie ran to the car and opened the door. "I'm so glad you can go, Trudy. Thank you, Mrs. Scuffer. We'll bring her home about six this evening."

"Bye, Mom," I said. "Love you." Katie and I ran into her house.

"Dad, Trudy's here," she said. "Let's go. I want to get Jinx settled in so he's not nervous."

We drove to Vicksburg for the rodeo, so it took us about an hour since her dad was pulling the horse trailer behind his truck.

"Katie tells me you want a horse," Mr. Wilson said.

"Yes, sir, but my dad says it would be too expensive."

"Well, he's right about that. Horses cost a lot. Katie's lucky that we have a free place to keep her horse."

As we pulled into the rodeo grounds, I gazed at the horse trailers and horses everywhere. Several girls ran up to Katie as we got out of the car.

"Hey, Katie," one of them said. "We've been looking for you. So glad you're here."

Even though I was dressed like they were, I didn't fit in. Katie introduced me but then they all went to prepare for the competitions, including Katie. Mr. Wilson went to help her get Jinx into a stall. I wasn't allowed to go with them. I saw a couple of Negro boys cleaning out trailers, but when they saw me, they looked the other way.

On the one hand, excitement welled up in me as the competition began, but I also longed to be on my own horse instead of watching. I tried to shake that longing. The events started with calf roping, bareback riding, and steer wrestling. Then it was time for barrel racing.

When it was Katie's turn, she galloped out and circled each barrel with ease. I knew how much she wanted to win. I cheered as loudly as I could. When all had competed, she had the best time, so she won first place. I jumped up and down clapping and yelling, and I forgot my longing and ran to give her a hug.

"You won!" I said. We hugged and she showed me her ribbon. People came by and yelled their congratulations and praise to Katie. Mr. Wilson smiled and patted Jinx on his back.

He squeezed Katie's hand. "Great job, gal. You showed them what a champion can do."

I wished Dad liked horses like Mr. Wilson.

Once Katie got Jinx cooled down, she handed me the saddle to put in the trailer while she carried other things. "Gosh, it's heavier than I thought," I said. I loved carrying it and imagined having my own one day. "Katie, when I was walking around, I saw some Negro boys cleaning the trailers. They wouldn't even speak to me. They looked the other way."

"Oh, they aren't allowed to speak to any of us. It's just understood. They're here to help, not to socialize. They could get in big trouble."

"Do you think that's right?"

"I don't know," she said. "It's just the way things are."

"I know it's been like this for a long time," I said, "but that's what the Freedom Riders, Martin Luther King Jr., Ruby Bridges, Mrs. Harvey, and my mom are trying to change."

"I don't know about all those other people," she said, "but the Freedom Riders are ending up in jail. Oh, here comes Dad. We better get ready to load Jinx."

Our conversation ended before I could tell her about meeting two of the Freedom Riders. I wasn't going to say anything in front of Mr. Wilson. He might be like Susan's stepdad, and I wanted Katie and me to stay friends.

On the way home, Katie and her dad talked about her next competition. Jealousy wrapped around me like a rope. I tried to think how nice it was to be able to go watch today, but it would have been perfect if I'd had a horse and had competed too. When we reached my house, Mom was waiting for me.

"Thanks for inviting me," I said to both Mr. Wilson and Katie. "I had such a good time."

"I loved having you go with me," Katie said. "Maybe you can go next time. I'll give you a call. Now that you have your cast off, we can go ride again at the stable."

I perked up at the mention of riding again. "That would be great," I said and got out of the car. When I got to the porch, I stood there with Mom and waved at Katie.

"Did you know the Negro boys working at the rodeo are not allowed to speak to any of the riders?" I said to Mom. "They just look the other way when you look at them."

"I'm not surprised. They must be careful around white

people because if they say something, they can be accused of being disrespectful."

"I don't think that's right. I want to be able to talk to Latrella, just like I talk to Jetta Mae."

"I understand that, Honey, but you don't want to put Latrella in any danger."

"What about you and Mrs. Harvey? You're friends. Are you putting her in danger?"

"It's different with adults. We're being careful where we go together, especially here in Jackson. Things are changing, but it takes time, and as I've told you before, some people are set on keeping things the same."

"Is Aunt Liz one of those people who want things to stay as they are?" I asked.

"No, but she has her work at the library that keeps her busy, and she's president of the PTA at Poindexter. She's involved in other things."

I knew Aunt Liz didn't like some of the things Mom was doing, but Mom wasn't going to tell me that. I decided to change the subject. "Thanks for letting me go with Katie. How was the scout meeting?"

"It was good. We talked about our service project for the year. There were several girls absent besides you. We only had eight there."

"What? We had eighteen girls last year." I couldn't believe that many were absent. I knew that one I had called had said she couldn't come because her dad didn't approve of Mom's work. "Did they quit because of what you're doing?" I asked.

"I don't know. No one said that to me or mentioned that they weren't coming. I guess we'll have to wait and see. Sarah

Jane and Polly were there. Sarah Jane asked where you were. You can call the girls who weren't there and remind them of our next meeting. Maybe Sarah Jane can help you."

"Sure," I said, but the last thing I wanted to do was to hear they couldn't come back because of what Mom was doing. And I doubted Sarah Jane would want to talk to me, much less help.

CHAPTER 25

THE NEXT FRIDAY Susan and I sat by each other in chorus. Her stepdad wasn't going to allow her to come to my house, but we could still be friends at school. If he knew Jetta Mae and saw how nice she was, he might feel differently, but Susan knew better. She said he would never change.

We started singing "Let there be Peace on Earth." When I sang the phrase "let it begin with me," I didn't know what I could do to create harmony in the world. All the turmoil going on was out of my control.

After school, we went out to practice tennis. Coach let me try out since my cast was off. Mom made me wait a week to strengthen my arm. Susan and I paired up together and started hitting balls back and forth. After warming up, we joined the others and Coach in the middle of the courts.

"I'd like to try some mixed doubles," he said. "It's always good to change around a little bit. You need experience with other members of the team. Let's do it by grade."

The seventh graders moved to one side, the eighth and ninth graders to the other. A guy asked Susan to be his partner, and I ended up with another guy.

"Are you good at tennis?" he asked.

"I think so." That seemed like a stupid answer, but I didn't know what else to say. I'd never played with a boy before, and my nerves kicked into high gear. We did some practice serves, volleyed a bit, and played one set.

The guy was a good tennis player. I missed a couple of shots, and he yelled,

"Come on, girl. Don't take your eye off the ball."

I tried to concentrate. We were a point ahead in the fifth game. One more point and we would win the set. The other team served, he returned it and then the ball was right in front of me. I hit it and thought it went out, but it landed on the line in the left corner.

"Nice!" he shouted. We'd won. We shook hands with the other players.

"What's your name?" he asked.

"Trudy. What's yours?"

He threw his racket in the air, caught it, and said, "I'm Brad. Good game. See ya around."

I ran to find Susan. She'd won her game also. And my arm had worked fine, thank goodness.

We waited together after practice. I loved dusk when the setting sun colored the sky rosy-pink. I stared at the changing colors. Susan's mom gave me a ride home.

That night, Mom and Dad wanted to go hear Medgar Evers speak. Mom said he was working hard to register Negroes to vote. The talk was at Jackson State.

Joseph and I sat down at the yellow kitchen table as Jetta Mae put plates of homemade spaghetti in front of us. I'd worked up an appetite playing tennis. Jetta Mae fixed her plate and stood at the counter eating.

"Jetta Mae, come sit down with us," I said. She just shook her head no. I continued, "We played a practice match at tennis today, and this guy Brad was my partner." I twirled my spaghetti around my fork.

"How did that go?" she said.

"Alright, I guess. He's a good tennis player. We won the practice game."

"Good for you."

Joseph sucked a noodle into his mouth while red sauce dripped down his chin.

"Use some manners," I said. "Don't be repulsive."

We finished eating, and I helped Jetta Mae with the dishes. Mom and Dad came into the kitchen, ready to go.

"Can we go with you, please?" I said. "I want to meet Medgar Evers. Jetta Mae could go too."

"I don't see why not," Mom said. "Would you like to go, Jetta Mae?"

"Yes, I'd like to hear him. Let me freshen up a bit, and if it's okay, I'll come along."

Dad frowned, but he didn't say no.

"Go wash your face, Joseph," Mom said. "I see spaghetti sauce on your chin."

When Jetta Mae came out of the house, she had on a jacket over her dress. She smiled and got into the back seat with Joseph and me. As we drove there, I wondered if Latrella would be there with her mom and dad and if people would notice Jetta Mae was with white people. After we got there and parked, we walked together with Mom and Dad leading the way to the auditorium.

"Do you see anyone you know?" Joseph asked Jetta Mae.

"Not yet," she said. I held her hand tight. The cool night air felt good on my face. Excitement stirred within me. It kind of felt like going to a football game. Negro boys and girls ran back and forth shouting and laughing. I didn't see any white children though.

Inside, Mrs. Harvey came over to Mom, hugged her, and said, "I'm so glad you came and brought your family." She patted my shoulder and smiled. Then she saw Jetta Mae and hugged her too.

Someone stepped to the podium, and everyone got quiet and took their seats. If there were other white people there, I couldn't see them, but to me it really didn't matter.

The president of Jackson State introduced Medgar Evers as the first field secretary for the NAACP. He said that Mr. Evers had served in the US Army and that he wanted to help promote fairness and equal rights for the Negro people.

"He wants the same thing Mom, Mrs. Harvey, and you want," I whispered to Jetta Mae.

Medgar Evers spoke in a manner so that people listened. He promoted action without any violence. He said it wasn't right that there were no Black police officers and firemen or any Black women employed as clerks and saleswomen even though the city had a 40% population of Black people. He wanted the schools to integrate so all children could get the best education. Loud clapping and cheers came from the crowd as he talked.

"Let's continue to register to vote and make ourselves heard," he said. "Let us promote love, not hate. Let us stand up for our race in a peaceful manner. Violence will only add to more violence. May God bless us all."

I'd searched the crowd to see if Latrella was there with her parents. It would have been great if we could have met up there. But there were so many people, I knew it was impossible to spot her. I did see a few white people as we were leaving.

"We better get going before it gets late," Dad said. "Jetta Mae's had a long day."

As we drove to Jetta Mae's, I tried to guess which house belonged to Latrella's grandmother. I knew she lived near the store, but I couldn't figure it out in the dark. They all looked the same.

"Bye," I said as Jetta Mae got out of the car. We drove off toward home.

"Dad, have you ever been friends with a Negro?" He looked over at me, then turned his eyes back on the road.

"I work with Colored men a lot on my jobs."

"I don't mean working friends. I mean like talking on the phone and going places together." I looked out the window at the houses again.

"No, I don't have any Colored friends like that. Why do you ask? Most white people and Colored people don't mix like that. Colored people aren't allowed in white restaurants."

"Would it be okay if I had a Negro friend like Mom has Mrs. Harvey?" I started to squirm.

"I'm not sure where you might meet a Colored child your age. Most people around here don't accept Colored children and white children playing together. It wouldn't be a safe thing right now."

"John Henry's your friend, isn't he, Dad?" Joseph said. "He brings our Christmas tree every year."

"Well, yes, he is, but he works for my company, so that is how I know him. Your mom knows Mrs. Harvey because of her work."

"What did you think about the meeting?" Mom asked Dad, putting an end to my questioning.

"Medgar Evers is young, but he's smart and he wants to help his people be able to vote and go to public places just like we do," Dad said. "I liked what he had to say. Because of my job, I can't be involved like you, but I do believe changes need to happen."

Dad's support for Mom made me feel better.

"I think the changes would be good for all Negroes," I said.

I knew I couldn't reveal my friendship with Latrella. Dad had said the same thing that Sarah Jane had said about not mixing. I didn't want to stop seeing Latrella. We'd have to keep it a secret unless I figured something else out.

"Dad, do you think I'll ever be able to have a horse?" I said. "I'd love to ride like Katie."

"Sweetie, I don't see that happening anytime soon. It costs a lot of money to take care of a horse, and finding a place to keep it is another expense."

"I could get a job and help pay for it."

Dad smiled and said, "Maybe someday." At least he didn't say a definite NO.

CHAPTER 26

WHEN WE GOT HOME, I noticed that Dad had put some dirt in the hole in the front yard. Pretty soon the leaves would cover the ground, and no one except us would know it was there. As soon as we got inside the house, I headed for my room, only to be stopped by Mom's voice.

"Why don't you go ahead and practice your piano?"

Not saying a word, I turned around and slid right onto the piano bench. I started playing the "Minuet in G." I messed up a couple of times but went back and tried again. I finally got it right. I didn't even mind the stupid metronome ticking away. Trying to let the music soothe me like it seemed to do for Mom, I closed my eyes as I played. It didn't soothe me in the least because I had to keep opening my eyes to see the notes.

"You've improved," Mom said. "You played that piece well. Practicing does pay off." Her compliment didn't take away my discomfort.

The phone rang, startling me. I answered, and it was Susan. "Hey, listen, Mom and I are taking the kids to the park tomorrow. Can you go with us? Dennis isn't going."

I checked with Mom, and she said I could go. I told Susan I would see her about one-thirty.

The next day I rode my bike over to Susan's. As we all got

THE END OF THE SIDEWALK

in their car, Susan and I started to sing "Old MacDonald Had a Farm." The kids laughed and sang along. At the park, while the kids played on the playground, Susan and I went over to the swings. I wanted to tell her about going to see Medgar Evers.

"I got to go to a rodeo with my friend Katie. She won first place in the barrel races. I had fun, but it made me want my own horse even more. Katie's lucky because her dad loves horses too."

"Do you think you'll ever get one?" she asked.

"I hope so, but it might not be until I grow up. Dad says we can't afford one now. My whole family went to Jackson State last night to listen to Medgar Evers. He pointed out that there are no Negro firemen or policemen or even garbage truck drivers. I didn't really know that."

"Better not say anything about it to Dennis or Mom. They think Medgar Evers is stirring up the Coloreds, and it isn't good. They think Whites and Coloreds should stay separate."

"Do you feel the same as they do?" I was curious to know if she believed like they did.

"I don't know. It's the way it's always been. I can see their point. But I see what your mom is saying too. I wish they would talk with her. They might see things differently. Hey, I'm thirsty. Let's go get a drink of water."

We ran across the street to the water fountain. There were two fountains just alike with signs above them. One said *Colored* and one said *White*.

"Do you think the water tastes any different?" she asked.

"Nope. I think it's silly to have two fountains, but some white people think they would get germs or something. I'll taste it and see." I started to bend down, and she grabbed me.

174

"Come on. Mom's going to be ready to go soon," Susan said. We walked back to the area where the children were playing.

"I was getting ready to call you two," her mom said. "We'd better get back. The baby needs a nap." Susan's mom jiggled him up and down.

When we got back to Susan's house, Mr. Sheridan stood at the door to greet them.

"What are you doing here?" he said to me. "Don't think I don't know who your mom is. She's trying to make trouble for us in Jackson."

"No, sir, she's trying to help get equal rights for everybody." I tried to act politely, but he frowned at me.

"Are you disputing my word, girl? Go on home now."

"Don't talk to Trudy like that," Susan said. "She's my friend."

I backed up toward my bike, lying on the ground.

He glared at her. "Excuse me, but do you know I'm the head of this household? Don't backtalk." Susan waved and turned to go in. I jumped on my bike, riding home like a streak in the wind. I was out of breath like I'd been running a race. Poor Susan. Her stepdad acted like a war general. Then I thought about Dad when the policeman brought me home. He'd spoken in a stern voice like Susan's dad had.

When I got home, I leaned my bike up against the garage and climbed up into Miss Magnolia. Hugging my knees to my chest, I thought about what he'd said about Mom. That was the same thing the policeman had said to her.

At supper, I had no appetite. My stomach hurt and Mom wasn't eating with us for some reason. As Dad said the blessing, I whispered a prayer for my friendship with Susan.

"Susan's stepdad doesn't want her to be my friend because he said Mom is making trouble," I said. "I tried to explain what Mom was doing, but he wouldn't listen."

"Honey, I'm sorry that happened," Dad said. "You and Susan can be just school friends for now."

"Yes, sir," I answered. Maybe I should have kept my mouth shut. I didn't want Susan blamed for what I'd said. I didn't want to put Latrella in any danger. And I wanted to make up with Sarah Jane. I really wanted to be friends with all of them, but I couldn't.

That night my bed was a welcome sight. As I turned out my light and climbed into bed, Mom peeked her head into the room.

"You asleep yet?" she said.

"No, ma'am." I guessed she was going to reinforce Dad's order, but instead, she sat down on my bed and took my hand.

"Your dad told me you tried to talk to Susan's stepdad. I want you to know that I appreciate you standing up for me. It takes courage for someone your age to say what you said. Mrs. Sheridan's glad that you and Susan are friends, but she needs Susan to help her. You keep on being a friend to Susan. We'll try to figure out a way you can do some things together outside of school." She rubbed my hand gently with hers. I didn't want her to stop.

"Thanks, Mom. I want people to understand what you're doing, but they're not interested in hearing my side."

Mom squeezed my hand, then kissed me on the cheek. "We must be patient and kind. Goodnight and sweet dreams."

It was the first time in a while that Mom had kissed me goodnight. I touched my cheek as if I could hold the kiss there.

CHAPTER 27

SIRENS WAILED in the distance but began sounding closer and louder. I sat straight up in bed. It was still dark outside. "Not again", I thought. It seemed like something happened almost every night. Running into Mom and Dad's room, I shook Mom awake.

"The fire trucks sound like they're coming to our house again. Why would they come now?"

"Honey, I imagine there's a fire somewhere," she said. "Go on back to bed." But Dad got out of bed as the lights flashed outside the window. Then Joseph came into the room.

"What's going on?" Joseph said. "I hear sirens out front."

Two fire trucks sped by, then a police car followed. The sirens screamed through the night. A real fire must be somewhere nearby.

"I'm going to see what's happening." Dad grabbed his robe and pulled it on. He lumbered down the hall with me following close behind.

"Can I go with you?" I asked.

"No sirree, you stay right here with your mom. I'll be back in a minute." When Dad opened the front door, I could smell smoke. "Stay put," he said as he disappeared down the sidewalk.

I stepped out onto the porch and looked toward the end of the sidewalk. My heart started pounding. The flashing lights looked like that was where they'd stopped. Was Latrella's grandmother's neighborhood on fire? I couldn't see much in the dark. The smoke smelled like our fires at Girl Scout Camp.

"Gertrude, get in this house right now," Mom said as she held on to Joseph.

I turned to see her holding Joseph close to her. "Mom, I'm worried about Latrella's grandmother and Jetta Mae. What if their houses are on fire? I want to go check." Tears rolled down my face.

"The police and firemen won't let anyone go close. Don't jump to conclusions. Wait until your dad gets back, and he'll tell us what he found out."

I went back inside the house. It seemed like Dad was gone for a long time. I prayed silently that Latrella's grandmother and my dear Jetta Mae were okay. I hoped Latrella was at her house with her parents. Sometimes she spent the night with her grandmother.

At last, Dad came in, shaking his head.

Joseph jumped up. "Did you see the fire? Was it big?" He danced around like his own pants were on fire.

"The Negro store burned. They suspect arson, but no one's certain. They got everyone out of the houses until they're sure the fire's contained."

"What's arson?" Joseph asked.

"That's when somebody sets a fire on purpose," said Dad.

"Why would anyone set the store on fire?" Joseph rubbed his hand through his hair.

"It's someone's way of scaring people and warning them to not try to change things," Dad said. "I hope they find out who did it, but I doubt they will." Dad shook his head. "Let's get back to bed now."

"Wait," I said. "Did the lady who owns the store get hurt? What about Jetta Mae and Latrella and her grandmother?" I pulled my nightgown close around me.

"What are you talking about?" Dad said. "Jetta Mae's house is down the road from the store. Who's Latrella? How do you know anyone who lives down there?" Dad looked surprised.

"Latrella's related to Jetta Mae," Mom said. "Trudy met her at the funeral."

"How do you know where she lives?" Dad asked.

I looked at Mom, hoping she would say something else, but when she didn't respond, I knew I had to answer Dad's question.

"Please don't be mad. Sometimes we meet in the woods, and I loaned her some books to read. She likes to read as much as I do. I went to the store one time looking for Latrella. She lives on another street, but sometimes she spends the night with her grandmother who lives near the store."

Staring at the floor, I waited for Dad to put me on restriction again.

"Look at me," he ordered.

I looked up and tried to focus on him, but my eyes blurred and I started crying.

Dad took a deep breath, and his broad shoulders heaved up and down. "Sweetheart, I know you're trying to be nice, but this is like going to see the Freedom Riders. You must talk to your mom or me before you do these things. You could jeopardize your safety and Latrella's even though you don't think you're doing anything wrong. That's why I made the boundary at the end of the sidewalk. It was for your protection."

"I'm sorry. But Latrella's my friend. She's smart and funny. Her dad's a professor at Jackson State, and her mom works there too. I've learned a lot from her."

THE END OF THE SIDEWALK

"You can't meet in the woods anymore. It's not safe."

"Your dad's not saying you can't get together with her at all," Mom said. "I'll talk to Jetta Mae, and we'll figure out something."

Dad frowned at Mom and said, "Let's hold off making any plans yet. We need to be careful about such get-togethers."

"I have her phone number," I said. "Can I call her?"

"No," Mom said. "I'll see that Jetta Mae gets word to Latrella's grandmother to tell her. Now we all need to get back to bed. It's late."

"Is it going to be like this the rest of my life?" I said. "I can't stand people who hate Negroes just because they have a different skin color."

"I hope not," Mom said, "but changes are hard for a lot of people here and in many places in the South. They're used to being in control. They think Negroes should do as they're told."

Joseph grabbed my arm. "I'll be your friend, Sis."

I hugged him. "I know I can count on you when you're home, but sometimes you're off playing with Frank or someone else."

"You can call me if I'm over there, and I'll come home right away."

"I think I want to be a Freedom Rider for Friendship," I said. "I want us to be friends with anyone, no matter where they're from or what color they are. I could ride up and down the streets singing 'make new friends, but keep the old, one is silver and the other is gold.'"

"Good idea, Trudy," Dad said. "We can talk more tomorrow, but now you need to get to bed like your mother said. Scoot." He squeezed my shoulders and pointed me down the hallway.

Joseph fell in behind me, whispering, "Can I sleep in your room tonight again?"

"Of course," I said and put my arm around his shoulder. "To tell you the truth, I sleep better when you're in there with me. Let's ask if Skipper can join us."

Mom and Dad agreed to let Skipper sleep in my room, and we settled in our beds. Joseph was asleep in no time, but I lingered awake thinking about Latrella and the fire.

CHAPTER 28

DAD DROPPED ME OFF at school early. I wanted to get my books and then go ask the librarian if she'd found information on Martin Luther King Jr. Down the hallway, I saw those two girls from the lunchroom. I looked down as I walked by so they wouldn't say anything, but that didn't work.

As I went by, one of them said in a loud voice, "Guess you're too stuck up to speak."

I turned around and said, "Oh, hi."

They both laughed, and one repeated what I said, real prissy like. Embarrassed, I hurried to my locker.

Wes came up behind me and said, "What are you doing here so early?"

"I'm going to the library to check on something."

"Can I walk with you?" he asked.

"Sure. The librarian was going to find me some information on Martin Luther King Jr. Have you heard about him?" Nervous about telling him for fear he might think I was stupid to be trying to learn about a Black man, I waited for his answer.

"I've heard of him. Isn't he a Negro preacher from Atlanta?"

"Yes," I said, surprised that he knew of him.

"I'd like to know more about him too." We walked to the library door, and he opened it for me to go in. My heart skipped a beat.

THE END OF THE SIDEWALK

In the library, I took a deep breath and tried to calm down. I went to the librarian to see if she'd found anything.

She smiled at me. "I did find a couple of newspaper articles, but you may find more at the main library downtown." She gave me copies of the articles. Wes and I sat down at a table, and we read about Martin Luther King Jr. and the bus boycott in Montgomery, Alabama. Not long after we finished reading, the bell rang, so we had to get to class.

"Thanks for sharing that info with me," he said. "I better get to my first period. See you in science lab." He strolled out of the library, and I think I floated to my English class. I liked Wes. Then I decided to ask Aunt Liz to take me to the main library. I could say I needed to do some research and just not say what it was about.

Wes nodded and grinned when I walked into science lab. I grinned back. I couldn't wait to tell Susan, but I'd have to do it when Wes wasn't around.

CHAPTER 29

AS SOON AS I got home from school, I rushed inside to tell Jetta Mae what had happened. Mom greeted me at the door smiling.

"I have some good news," she said. "Jetta Mae and I have been rejoicing all afternoon."

"What? What?" I asked, excited to hear her good news.

Mom's eyes lit up. "The Interstate Commerce Commission ruled that all signs that say *White* or *Colored* in public places must come down by November first, thanks to the Freedom Riders who persisted in their non-violent protests to get the law changed."

"What is the Interstate Commerce Commission?" I'd never heard of it before.

"It's a government agency that sets up rules for travel on railroads and buses. The ruling ends segregation in waiting rooms and on buses. The ruling also includes lunch counters, like at Woolworth's or drugstores." Mom smiled again.

"I'm happy because I think this is a step in the right direction."

"Does that mean Jetta Mae can use the bus front door and can sit wherever she wants?" I asked.

"Yes. Maybe not tomorrow, but change has come for sure. Oh, and Jetta Mae has a surprise for you in the kitchen."

THE END OF THE SIDEWALK

"That's great news, Mom." After throwing my books on the bed in my room, I rushed out to the kitchen. "What's the surprise, Jetta Mae? Butterscotch pie?"

Jetta Mae wiped her hands on a towel. The kitchen smelled of good food. A plate of pork chops sat on top of the stove. She smiled and put her hands on her hips.

"Trudy, what are you talking about?" she said.

"Mom said you had a surprise for me. Is it a butterscotch pie?"

"No, it's better than that." She opened the pantry door. Out jumped Latrella. I grabbed her in a hug.

"Is Big Mama okay?" I said. "I know the fire must have been scary."

"Scary isn't the word for it," Latrella said. "We were terrified. My mom and dad couldn't reach her at first. After the fire trucks left, we were able to go get her. She stayed at our house last night, and it was so late that my mom let me stay home with her today. Big Mama says she's going to move. I hope she moves in with us."

"Come on, let's go to my room. I have something to tell you." We went down the hall and sat down on my bed. "When the fire happened," I said, "I was so worried that something would happen to you and Big Mama. I said your name and Dad wanted to know who I was talking about. I told him about you and about us meeting in the woods." I saw her frown.

"Now why did you have to tell him? That was our secret."

"I was scared. I had to tell the truth. He didn't get mad, but he said we couldn't meet anymore in the woods, that it wasn't safe."

"Most everyone thinks the Klan set the store on fire," Latrella said. She put her hands on her hips, staring at me with her big dark eyes.

"My dad thought that too. He's thinking of both of us and our safety." I stared right back at her.

"Don't go getting sad on me. I need a new book. I finished *Misty of Chincoteague*." She tugged on my arm. "Come on. I don't want to be sad now. Perk up."

"Okay. I looked for you the other night at Jackson State. We went to Medgar Evers's talk. There were so many people there."

"My dad was there. I would have gone with him if I'd known you were going to be there. Why didn't you call me?" She looked at me with disappointment written all over her face.

"My parents decided at the last minute to take us with them, and Jetta Mae went too. Did you know that Jetta Mae dreams of owning a bakery someday?"

"No, I didn't know that about Auntie Jetta, but I'm upset I didn't know about you going to Jackson State. I'm sure my dad would have let me go if I'd asked him. How was it?"

"There weren't many white people there, but Mr. Evers said some things that I didn't even realize about Black men not being hired for jobs like firemen and policemen. He also said that Black women can only get cleaning jobs and can't be a salesperson in a store. I think that's a shame."

"Tell me about it. Now you know what I deal with all the time. I try to think about being a doctor, but I might not be able to get in medical school unless I go up north. I need to make top-notch grades from now until I graduate. Maybe I can get a scholarship."

"I know you're smart. I feel certain you can do it. You make better grades than I do."

"Yes, but you aren't Black, so it will be easier for you wherever you go." She frowned.

"Hey, listen, do you think you could find any information on Dr. Martin Luther King Jr.? I checked in the library at my school, and so far, the librarian gave me just two articles. I want to read more about him."

"I'll check, but if you don't have it, I'm sure we don't. Your school's library is much better than mine. That's why I've been borrowing your books."

"We have to leave in about thirty minutes," Jetta Mae called to us, "so you two get your book swapping done."

"Here's another good horse book titled *King of the Wind*." I handed it to her and put *Misty* back on my shelf. I sat down on my bed, and she sat in my desk chair across from me.

"Guess what?" I said. "This guy named Wes went to the library with me. We read together those articles about Martin Luther King Jr., and Wes wanted to know about him too. He's in my science lab class.

"Is he your boyfriend?" she said and smiled.

"No, but he's nice and he's cute. Oh, and these two girls who've been teasing me passed me in the hall. I looked down, and they called me stuck up. I then said hi, and they repeated what I said in a sassy sort of way. I just ignored them, but I was embarrassed."

"You did the right thing so you shouldn't be embarrassed."

"Latrella, it's time to go," Jetta Mae called.

Time had gone by so fast. Latrella and I hugged. I didn't know when I would see her again. We'd have to figure something out.

After they left, I called Susan. Mr. Sheridan answered the phone, and I almost hung up. I was hoping he wouldn't be at home.

"May I speak to Susan, please?" I twirled the black cord in my hand.

"Who is this?" he asked in a gruff voice.

"This is Trudy."

"No, you can't speak to her. Don't call here anymore. I don't want her associating with you. Your family is supporting the wrong people." He hung up.

I stood there, staring at the black receiver in my hand. Why did he have to be so mean?

"What are you doing?" Mom asked. I put the receiver back into the cradle.

"Susan's dad hung up on me. He won't let me talk to her. He says we're supporting the wrong people. I hate him." Feeling sorry for myself, I started back to my room.

"Come here for a minute," Mom said. "I want to talk to you."

She sat down in the rocker in the living room, and I slid onto the couch, grabbing a throw pillow to put in my lap.

"When I was a little girl," she said, "there were some Negroes who lived down the road from our house. My dad told us to never go down there because they were dirty. I didn't understand what he meant, but I was curious. So, one day, I walked down that way, and I saw a Negro girl watching me. I nodded at her, and she turned and ran. She didn't look dirty at all. I realized when I got older that my dad just didn't want me talking to any Negroes."

My eyes grew wide with amazement. "Granddaddy was against integration?"

"Yes, he was, and he disagreed with me often on my ideas. Last year when I went to a church meeting in Chicago, I found out that many of the church groups there were integrated. I thought that there shouldn't be any reason why we couldn't do that here if they were doing it, so I brought the idea back to my groups here.

Some were for it, but not all agreed. Some think violence is the way to control people who are speaking out for equal rights. I don't think so, do you?"

"No, I don't. I don't like people talking mean about you. I know it's not true, but it hurts to hear them say such awful things. Now that I know Latrella and Mrs. Harvey, I like them, and Jetta Mae is the best. She says that we're all God's children, and she's right."

"We are. Before I got on the commission, your dad and I talked about it. I knew I would be disliked by some, but I didn't know all the things that would happen because of it. I don't want you saying you hate somebody because of how they believe. That isn't going to help. The governor is for segregation and is against the commission, but I don't hate him."

"I wish more people were on your side."

"I do, too, and I think there will be in time."

"Do you think you and Aunt Liz will ever be friends again? I miss them coming to supper." I squirmed on the couch because I thought it was a touchy subject.

"Your Aunt Liz and I are still friends. We don't have to agree on everything, but we love each other, and that will never change. Our busy schedules have interfered with us having supper."

"Mom, I know Aunt Liz is upset. She doesn't want Frank or Sarah Jane coming over to play. She acts strange when I go over there and not at all like she used to. Sarah Jane spends time with Polly rather than with me, and Polly doesn't like me."

"I'm sorry that things have changed for you, but I believe it will get better. Sarah Jane will be here soon for her piano lesson. Maybe you can talk afterward."

Later, when the chords from the piece "Aragonaise" from the opera of Carmen drifted down the hall, I could picture Mom sitting there with her eyes closed and a smile on her face. I couldn't help but wish I could play as well as Sarah Jane. After the music stopped, I rushed into the living room.

"Can you stay for a little while?" I asked Sarah Jane.

"No, I still have some homework left to do," she said. I frowned at Mom, but she smiled and straightened the bench.

"I'll walk with you home then," I said as I followed her out the back door. "Can we stop for a few minutes in Miss Magnolia?"

"I guess so," she said. "I can't stay long. I have a good bit to do."

Once we settled in the tree, I told her about the fire.

"We heard the fire engines," she said. "Mom thought they might be going to your house again."

"I thought the same thing. I miss you. We hardly ever get together anymore. Are you mad at me? I'm sorry for what I said about you and Polly."

Out of the blue, she started crying.

"What's the matter?" I scooted up close to her and put my arm around her.

"I've been mean to you. All these things have been happening. You've never gotten mad at me or yelled at me." She sobbed.

"It's okay," I said. "I know it's hard when your mom and my mom don't agree. We need to figure out a way to get them back together."

"No, it's not okay. Don't even say that. You're my best friend forever and ever. I'm sorry for the way I've acted. Polly is a good friend, but she'll never take your place. Never."

THE END OF THE SIDEWALK

"I feel the same way. I like Susan and Katie and Latrella, but they can't take your place as my best friend." Tears rolled down my cheeks.

Sarah Jane wiped her tears away with her hand. "What are you crying about?"

"What about Mom and the commission? Won't your mom still stop you from coming over and doing things with me?"

"I think she'll let me. She believes Colored people need equal rights, but she's scared of the repercussions, or at least that's what she tells me. She loves you, and she wants us to be friends."

We sat there, wrapped in the evening shadows. The crickets chirped, and I thought they chirped a happy song for us. Before Sarah Jane and I climbed down, we hooked pinkies and laughed. As she walked off, I turned and ran back into the house. I wanted to shout for joy.

"Mom," I called.

"I'm in my office."

I went back to her office where she sat at her desk, letters stacked in front of her. "Sara Jane and I made up."

"That's wonderful," she said. "See? I told you." She started sorting through her mail.

"Now you and Aunt Liz need to make up."

"What are you talking about?"

"You told me how you have different opinions from the Governor and Susan's dad but would still talk to them. You and Aunt Liz don't talk like you used to. You need to tell her you aren't mad at her." I'd said it fast, so I didn't lose my courage.

"I'm not mad at Aunt Liz. We do have differing opinions, and I can't change that."

"You're still sisters, and I want them to eat with us like they used to. We can get together and talk about other things, can't we?"

"I'll talk to her and invite them over, but I can't promise she'll come."

"Okay."

I went to practice my piano, thinking I'd have to keep asking Mom if she'd talked to Aunt Liz. I sat down and played Beethoven's "Fur Elise" without any mistakes. I felt like dancing back to my room.

CHAPTER 30

SITTING ON THE FENCE, I rubbed Whisper's mane as he crunched the carrot I had brought him. I hadn't visited him since I got my cast off three weeks ago. I wished I could climb onto his back and ride through the pasture without a care in the world. It was a great dream, but not a possible one.

He stamped his foot for more snacks.

"Sorry, buddy, I don't have any more. I'll bring two next time." I gave him one more pat and hopped down. I thought about walking up the long driveway to the house to see if they would let me help with the horses but decided I should get permission from Mom and Dad first. I had done enough things without permission, and I wanted Dad to know I could be responsible.

After heading to Sarah Jane's, Aunt Liz said she was over at Polly's. I should have known that *was* where she would be. Even though we'd made up, she was still friends with Polly.

"Aunt Liz, could you take me to the library downtown with you one day? I need to look up something."

"You can't find it at the school library?" she asked.

"No, the librarian said I might find it downtown in some newspapers there."

"I could take you Saturday, if that's okay." She smiled at me.

"That would be great. Thanks." I started to leave.

"I'll pick you up at ten o'clock."

I ran back and gave her a hug. "I'll be ready."

I skipped all the way home and ran through the back gate where Skipper met me. Then he ran over to Miss Magnolia and started sniffing around the bottom of the trunk.

"*Psst*, come here," someone said. I looked up in the tree, and there sat Latrella.

"What are you doing here?" I said. "Does Jetta Mae know you're here?" I climbed up to join her.

"No, I walked down the street like I might be going to the bus stop. When I got to your house, I checked to see if anyone was looking, and I dashed into the backyard, so here I am."

I frowned at her. "You shouldn't be here." The fire and what Dad had said made me realize it wasn't a smart thing to do.

"I know we can't meet anymore in the woods, but I wanted to return your book. I'm pretty sure Big Mama is going to move in with us. We have a spare bedroom, so she'll like that. And guess what? Mom said I could call you if it's okay with your parents. I better go." She gave me a hug, jumped out of the tree, and disappeared. I ran out front to see if I saw her, but she was nowhere in sight.

On Saturday, Aunt Liz picked me up at ten o'clock sharp. When we got to the library, she took me to the room with the big microfilm machines. We didn't have those machines in my school library. She left me there and went back to the desk. An older girl was on one of the machines.

"Could you help me find something about Martin Luther King Jr.?" I asked.

"Did you check the card catalog or the encyclopedia?"

I went and checked both. I did find something in the encyclopedia. It told about him and the Montgomery Bus Boycott, like the newspaper article I'd gotten at school, and it also had some interesting facts about him. I wrote down everything. I also found one newspaper article about his founding of the Southern Christian Leadership Conference. Then I went to find Aunt Liz.

"Did you find what you were looking for?" she asked. She'd been helping to shelve books even though she wasn't working that day.

"Yes, ma'am. Thanks for bringing me." We rode along in silence for a while. I worked up some courage to ask a few questions.

"Do you like Negroes?"

She started rubbing the steering wheel with her thumb. "I don't know many Colored people, but I don't have anything against them. I like Jetta Mae."

"Do you think we should be friends with them and not treat them so bad? Why can't they use this library?"

She frowned. "We have certain rules here, and we must follow them. They have their own library. Let's talk about you. When is your first tennis match?"

"I'm not sure. I'll let you know when I'm going to play. Maybe you can come." She nodded as she pulled up in front of my house. Aunt Liz had made it clear that she didn't want to talk about Negroes. "Thanks again," I said as I got out of her car.

The phone rang as soon as I walked into the house. I answered it and said, "Scuffer residence."

A voice sang, "Three-five-three-dash-six-seven-five-six."

Latrella and I both laughed.

"Is it alright that I called?" she asked.

THE END OF THE SIDEWALK

"Yes. I just came back from the library. I got some information on Martin Luther King Jr., and I'm going to do a report on him."

"That's great. I want to read it when you finish."

"What are you going to be for Halloween?" I asked. "We could trick or treat together if your costume covered you up."

"I'm not going to be anything but myself. How about you?"

"Mom doesn't believe in store-bought costumes, so I'm dressing as Annie Oakley."

"Who's she?" she asked.

"She was a cowgirl, and she could ride a horse and shoot a gun as good as any man. She was famous."

"Are you going to carry a gun?" she asked.

"A wooden one Dad made for me, not anything real for sure. Why aren't you going to wear a costume? I want us to go trick or treating together."

"Nope. It's not safe for me. Word's out on the street that we need to stay in after dark so no white folks can blame us for anything."

"Why don't you go with me? I could loan you a costume. I have a clown costume Mom made a couple of years ago, and there is a mask and a wig."

"Nope. I'm staying put. In the daytime I can see people, but at night, it's different. Maybe someday things will change, but for now, I'm not going to take that kind of chance."

I knew she was right, but it didn't seem fair at all. I thought she might trick or treat in her own neighborhood. "I tell you what. I'll split my candy with you and get Jetta Mae to bring it to you. I get way more than I need."

"You don't have to do that. I'm used to these restrictions. Someday it will be different."

"I know I don't have to, but I want to, so that's that."

"Thanks, three-five-three-dash-six-seven-five-six," she sang into the phone.

We laughed and said goodbye, but I had an icky feeling about her missing out on trick or treating.

On Halloween, I went trick-or-treating with Sarah Jane, Polly, Frank, and Joseph. Sarah Jane dressed as Snow White, Polly as a gypsy, Frank as a baseball player, and Joseph as a doctor. Joseph wore one of Dad's white shirts, and Mom had bought a play stethoscope, which he wore around his neck.

We went to several houses, and right before we reached the end of the sidewalk, lots of kids ran by us shouting Trick or Treat. We yelled back to them and laughed. We used flashlights because it was black as burnt campfire logs and a little spooky. Joseph held my hand as we went from door to door.

"You look like a real cowgirl," Polly said. "I like your bandana."

"Thanks, I like your outfit too. Maybe you can tell my fortune when we get back." For once, Polly was nice to me. Had Sarah Jane told her what I'd said? I hoped not.

After a while, Sarah Jane, Polly, and Frank walked ahead as we started toward home. Someone came up behind me, poking something in my back.

"Put your hands in the air and give me your bag of candy," he said.

It was a boy dressed like the Lone Ranger. He had on a mask. His friend was dressed like Tonto, the Lone Ranger's companion. Before anyone could grab my bag, I took off running toward my house.

Joseph yelled, "Leave my sister alone." He followed me.

We ran so fast that I was out of breath when we reached the house. Sarah Jane and the other two sat on the steps.

"What happened?" Sarah Jane asked.

"Some boy tried to steal our candy."

Joseph pulled on my shirt. "I dropped my stethoscope. Let's go find it."

"Heck, no. Those guys might still be lurking out there. I'll look for it tomorrow." I didn't want to take any chances meeting up with them again.

The candle burned in the Jack-o-lantern on the front step. The streetlights glowed. It was getting late.

"We're heading home," Sarah Jane said. "We had fun."

"Happy Halloween," I said. "See you tomorrow."

"Well, how was it?" Mom asked after we went inside. "It looks like your bags are full."

"Some guy almost stole our candy," Joseph said, "but we ran so fast he couldn't catch us. I dropped my stethoscope though. Trudy said she would look for it tomorrow."

"Honey, do you know who it was?" Mom asked me.

"No, we got away from them too fast."

"You two better get ready for bed. It's getting late."

"Okay, Mom. Is Dad home yet?"

"Yes, he's back at his desk. You two can go check in with him before you go to bed. Why don't you go show him your costumes?"

We ran back to see Dad.

"Wow," Dad said when we went into the room. "I see my cowgirl and Dr. Joseph Scuffer. Those costumes look perfect for you two."

"I'm Annie Oakley. See, I used the gun you made for me. Now if I just had a horse, I'd be all set."

"And where do you think you would keep your horse? In the backyard?" he asked.

"I haven't figured that out yet, but I'm working on it."

Dad laughed and gave us both a hug.

When I got in my room, I poured out my candy and started dividing it up for me and for Latrella. Now I knew she'd made the best decision. What if she'd been with us and those boys had found out who she was? That would have been awful. I counted out twenty pieces for her and twenty for me, got a brown bag, wrote her name on it, and put her candy in it. I fell right to sleep when I got in bed.

Ding-dong, ding-dong, ding-dong.

It was another night interruption. In the backyard, Skipper barked and howled like a wolf.

Dad yelled, "Get that dog in right now." He headed toward the front door with Mom right behind him. I ran to let Skipper in. When I got back to the living room, Dad was peering out the door into the night.

"Stupid fools," he said. "Who's out there? It's two o'clock in the morning." He turned to me and said, "Go get a flashlight." I ran to the kitchen and grabbed off the table the flashlight that we'd used for trick-or-treating.

When I got back to Dad, he took it and shone the bright light into the yard. It was quiet and still.

"All right," he said as he came inside. He shut the door. "No one's out there. Let's get back to bed. Just some pranksters disturbing our sleep."

"Can Skipper sleep in my room?" I said. "Please, just this time."

"I guess so, but hurry and get back in bed."

Back in my room with Skipper, I pulled him close to my bed. I knew he would bark if anyone came into the backyard. Still, I made sure my windows were shut. I didn't want to take any chances. Joseph sneaked in to sleep with me again.

I heard Dad say, "June, I'm sick and tired of all these interruptions at night. Can't your committee do something about it?"

"My committee has no authority like that," she said. "But change is happening. We knew it wouldn't happen overnight."

I heard their door close. I'd had enough excitement for one night. I would think they had too. I prayed they wouldn't argue anymore.

CHAPTER 31

IN SCIENCE LAB the next day, Susan turned to me and said, "Girl, why didn't you call me? I thought we might meet up and trick or treat together."

"Your stepdad told me not to call you anymore, and I didn't want him to get mad at you or me. Mom said to wait for you to call me. We'll work something out. I'm sorry."

She made a face at me but Coach started calling the roll so we couldn't talk anymore until after class. When the bell rang, I started telling her about the doorbell ringing at two o'clock in the morning.

She grabbed my arm. "Oh my gosh. Weren't you spooked?"

"Yes. Dad said it was probably because of that ICC ruling. People are angry about it and want to blame Mom and others who support Negroes."

"What's the ICC?" she asked.

"It's the Interstate Commerce Commission." I explained to her about the signs saying *Colored* and *White* on bathrooms and waiting rooms were now not legal and would need to be taken down. It would mean Negroes wouldn't have to use separate entrances or bathrooms.

"Boy, Dennis isn't going to like that," Sarah said. "I bet he won't be use public restrooms anymore. He said we weren't moving to that house on your street either. He's hardheaded about his beliefs. Okay, got to get to class." She moved quickly down the hall.

For the rest of the day, my mind kept returning to the ICC ruling and what might happen because of it. After school, I hurried home to talk to Jetta Mae.

Mom was teaching a piano lesson, so I tiptoed through the living room and darted into the kitchen for some time with Jetta Mae before she had to leave.

"Hi. You're like a ray of sunshine in my day," she said.

"Thanks, say, do you know if they took any signs down yet?"

"I haven't put my mind on that today. I imagine some took them down right away, but most people here will take a while to adjust to it. Some will refuse to accept the new rules, saying they don't apply yet. I'm not betting on it happening overnight."

"Mom says once the signs are gone, you can sit where you want on the bus, drink out of any water fountain, and use any restroom."

"I'm not trying it out right away. I think it's better to ease into it. Some people make me mighty uncomfortable with hateful stares and mutterings loud enough that I can hear what they're saying." Jetta Mae wiped her brow with her little towel.

"Those people don't know what a great person you are, or they wouldn't say mean things" I perched on a stool close to her.

"Not many white people want to get to know the likes of me, sweet girl. Can you put these things in your mom's room for me?"

"Yes, I will." I picked up the basket of clothes. "I guess she told you about last night."

"Your mom did tell me. Lord knows, some people think they have nothing better to do with themselves than try and stir up trouble."

"I wish Dad could have caught them. He would have told them a thing or two."

"It's just as well he didn't. They're not the kind of people who would listen. Don't worry. Their tactics aren't going to stop the changes. They'll have to follow the laws set up by our country, not their laws, but they'll resist as long as they can. Now get those clothes put away and save some chattering for later."

"Okay." I laughed.

"Take your giggles and run."

Jetta Mae kept her cheery attitude no matter what. I thought she'd like to show people, like that man who pushed in front of her at the bus stop, that now she could sit wherever she liked.

As I put some clothes in Mom and Dad's room, I saw an open letter on Dad's desk. I hesitated to look, but it was different from the others Mom had received. The words on it weren't handwritten. They'd been cut out of a magazine and pasted on the paper. Since it was wide open, I couldn't resist. The pasted words said, YOU ARE A DISGRACE TO MISSISSIPPI. GET OUT OF JACKSON IF YOU KNOW WHAT'S GOOD FOR YOU.

Anger riled up in me, But I couldn't act like I knew about it. Mom had already warned me about doing something without permission. Still, I looked at it again and noticed that no one had signed it.

I didn't think Mom and Dad would consider moving, but I knew Dad was going to be furious when he saw the letter.

When he got home late, we were already eating supper. He went to the bedroom to put his things away, then he brought the letter to the table.

THE END OF THE SIDEWALK

"When were you going to tell me about this letter?" he asked Mom, shaking it in the air.

"After supper, I thought we could discuss it. That's why I put it on your desk." she answered as she wiped her mouth with her napkin. "Please calm down."

"This letter is a threat. I've had my fill of this trash."

"I don't want to talk about this in front of the children," she said in a soft voice.

Dad said firmly, "We need to talk about it with the children They've been right in the middle of all this harassment. No one's going to run us out of town, but I tell you, I'm sick of the letters and constant attacks."

"Please don't be so loud. They're trying to make me quit," Mom's voice quivered. "I can't let them get their way. I must keep trying."

Joseph and I sat there, not saying a word. We knew to not interfere. I squirmed in my seat.

"Listen to this," Dad said, then read the letter to us.

"I don't want to move," Joseph said.

"Let's go into the living room so we can talk more about this," Dad said.

We left our supper and followed him. Dad sat in the rocking chair, and Mom took the chair beside him. Joseph and I sat on the couch.

"What do you know about slavery?" Dad asked us.

"I know a long time ago Negroes were brought here from Africa," I said. "They were captured and brought over to be slaves for the white people. They worked on the plantations and picked cotton."

"That's right, but it wasn't that long ago. It started in the United States hundreds of years ago, but it only ended ninety-six years ago.

That may seem like a long time, but it's not so long when you know how long it went on. The slaves were treated terribly. Their owners would buy and sell them, even separating families. The owners made them work very hard in horrible conditions. Slaves weren't free to do anything. If they tried to escape, they were punished and sometimes killed. Slavery caused a war between the states, the North and the South, when Abraham Lincoln was President."

"I know about Abraham Lincoln," Joseph said. "His picture is on the penny." He ran to his room and brought back a penny. He showed it to me as if I didn't already know, but I smiled and nodded.

"Didn't Abraham Lincoln give the Gettysburg Address?" I asked. "We have to memorize it this year in history class. We learned that the North was called the Union and the South was called the Confederacy. My teacher said there was a park in Vicksburg where they fought."

"Yes, that's right," Dad said. "Lincoln and lots of other people didn't believe in slavery. The North won the war, and an amendment to the US Constitution was supposed to end slavery. But many white people still held power over the former slaves. Those white people didn't think of Negroes as equal, took away many of their privileges, and still treated them as slaves. Whites wanted to live separately in every way and continued to hurt and kill Negroes for doing things without giving them any chance to tell their side. In the South, white people made their own laws, and it was hard for the Negroes to make money."

"Is that what they call the Jim Crow laws?" I asked.

"Yes. For example, if a white man was coming down the sidewalk, a Black man was expected to cross the street and walk on the other side. White men and women called Negroes terrible names and made them scared for their lives."

"People like the Freedom Riders and Medgar Evers are speaking out for their Civil Rights," Mom added. "I want them to have the same rights that we have. That's why I'm on the commission."

"We're upset about the phone calls and the letters with threats," Dad said, "but the people doing this aren't brave." He held up the letter and shook it. "They think they're better and smarter, but we don't think so. Your mother and I will take care of you, and we don't want you to be afraid. If someone says something mean to you, you should tell us. It's best to ignore them, but we can discuss it. Do you have any questions?"

Mom looked at my dad and smiled.

"Nobody's said anything to me," Joseph said. "That boy did try to take our candy at Halloween, but we outran him. Did you fight in that war, Dad?"

"No, it was way before I was born." Dad chuckled. "I may be old, but I'm not over a hundred years old."

"Well, some girls say things to me," I said, "but I try to do what you and Jetta Mae said about ignoring them."

"I tell you what," Dad said. "Let's have a little prayer." Dad took Mom's hand, and she reached for mine. I grabbed Joseph's, and we made a circle. Dad said, "Lord, protect our family. Give us courage to stand for what is right and to help our country be a place for all people to enjoy freedom. Amen."

We all hugged each other. It was a great moment.

After Dad's talk, I made a trip to Miss Magnolia. I snuggled into my favorite spot and breathed in the cool night air. The stars were sprinkled across the dark sky, twinkling like hundreds of tiny candles. Lightning bugs flashed around in the night air. It reminded me of Girl Scout Camp when we would walk to our cabin at night.

Skipper put his front feet up on the trunk of the tree, barked at me, and wagged his tail. I laughed as I climbed down.

"You want some attention, Skip?" I rubbed his fur back and forth. He licked my hand. "Let's ask Mom if you can sleep in my room again tonight." I ran up the back steps with Skipper close behind.

CHAPTER 32

I WALKED ACROSS our front yard, the leaves crunching under my feet. The yard looked like a puffy brown quilt with black threads sticking up all over. The almost-bare pecan trees had let go of their leaves, blanketing our yard with dead leaves. I spun my tennis racket around in my hand. Susan and I had been practicing after school for the last two weeks.

"I'm home," I yelled as I stepped inside the door.

"Shhh," Mom said, waving her hand at me. One of her students was playing the piano.

"Oops, sorry," I whispered as I scooted by, depositing my books on the table before going to see Jetta Mae. She was working late to get things ready for Thanksgiving tomorrow. I had promised I would help her today when I got home from school.

"Now what can I do to help?" I said as I wrapped my arms around Jetta Mae's big middle and gave her a hug.

"Well, you can get busy cracking some pecans for the pie."

Joseph and I had been collecting pecans from our yard. I grabbed the nutcracker, sat down at the yellow table, and pulled some nuts from a bag. "You remember how you told me about Martin Luther King Jr.?" I said as I cracked the first pecan's shell.

"Yes, I do. He's a mighty fine preacher."

THE END OF THE SIDEWALK

"Aunt Liz took me to the library a while back, and I looked up some information on him. He's so smart that he started college when he was fifteen. He also believes, like the Freedom Riders, to protest without violence. You told me about him helping with the bus boycott in Montgomery, Alabama. I wish he would come here and do a bus boycott. Did you know it lasted more than a year, but it worked there?"

"Child, why are you so concerned about the buses? I don't want me a stitch of trouble."

"Why do you think you'll get in trouble?" I asked. "It's a law now."

"Not everybody sees it that way. They can turn a situation around so it looks like I'm doing something wrong. I've had it happen before, and I don't want to rouse anyone."

"What happened before?" I asked as I pulled out more pecans to shell.

Jetta Mae looked serious. "My dad was hauling something for a white man, and I went with my dad. I was about fifteen. While Dad was loading the stuff in his truck, the man spanked my backside. When I yelled at him, Dad came running. I told Dad what happened, and the man laughed. He said, 'Now Mr. Green, you know I'm a gentleman, and I wouldn't do anything like that. Your daughter's mighty haughty trying to get me in trouble. You better tell her to mind her manners.'" Jetta Mae had spoken in a deep voice to imitate the man.

"My dad frowned and shook his head at me," she continued in her normal voice. "Then he said 'yes sir,' to the man. I went and got in the truck, but when Dad started to get in, the man slapped him on the back, almost knocking him down, and he said, 'Green, you better reprimand your daughter for insulting me.' Dad got out of the car and came around to my door. He pulled me out and shook me hard, telling me to apologize that instant. I looked down at the ground, but he shook me again. My dad had never talked to me like that, so I looked at the man and said I was sorry. On the way home, my dad told me he knew I was telling the truth, but he didn't want to make trouble." Jetta Mae looked at me with sadness in her eyes. "I do my best now to not stir things up. I want to live in peace."

"Does Mom know about that?" I asked as took out more pecans to crack as fast as I talked.

"No, that was a long time ago," she said. She picked up the turkey and held it up in the air. "Isn't this a pretty bird? He must weigh twenty pounds."

It didn't look the least bit pretty to me. I didn't even like to think about it being alive at one time. "It's really big," I said. I knew she was trying to change the subject, but I was still bothered by her story. "You should tell Mom about that white man. Maybe her commission could do something."

"Now listen, that happened long ago. Anyway, it's Thanksgiving. Let's think of all the things we should be thankful for."

"I'm thankful for you," I replied.

I heard someone coming up the back steps. I peered out the back door, and to my surprise there stood Latrella.

"Hey, what's going on?" I said. "How'd you get here?" I pulled her into the kitchen. She hadn't heeded my warning about walking by herself down our street or Sarah Jane's. She had a stubborn streak for sure.

"How'd you think?" she asked. "I walked here."

"From the end of the sidewalk?"

THE END OF THE SIDEWALK

She set a book on the table and rubbed her hands on her arms back and forth. "It's getting chilly. I came the back way and hid behind bushes when I saw someone. I wanted to see you. Big Mama's moving next week, and since we can't meet anymore, I brought your book back. Thanks for letting me borrow all of them."

"How come she's moving so soon? I thought it wouldn't be for several months." I stared at her in disbelief. "I'm going to miss you. I wish things were different. It's not fair. Just when we were getting to know each other so well, and now we can't see each other." My lip quivered.

"I'll miss you, too, but I'm glad Big Mama is moving because it's not safe there anymore. You're the nicest white person I know."

She squeezed my hand and tears rolled down my cheeks. I didn't try to stop them.

"You want to keep one book? I have plenty," I said.

"What about *King of the Wind*? I love that one," she said. She wiped her face and moved closer to me.

"Sure." I handed the book back to her.

She pulled it to her chest. "Oh, thank you so much. It's my favorite of all."

"Now you girls cheer up," Jetta Mae said. "Put smiles on your faces." She took all the nuts I'd shelled and got busy preparing the pecan pie.

Latrella and I sat there and talked for a bit. Having finished her piano lessons, Mom came into the kitchen. "Latrella, how did you get here?"

Latrella wiped her face again with her hands and smiled at Mom as if nothing was wrong. "Mrs. Scuffer, I had to see Trudy. Big Mama's moving in with us, so I don't know when I'll ever see her again. I brought her book back to her, but now I need to get back because I didn't tell Big Mama where I was going."

"No, we'll take you to her house. I don't want you walking out there by yourself."

"I'll be fine, and I don't want to put you to any trouble," Latrella said as she started out the back door.

"Stop right now," Mom said sternly. "We're taking you home. You and Gertrude go get in the car. Jetta Mae, are you ready to go?" Mom asked.

"Yes. All you have to do with this pretty bird is stick it in the oven tomorrow. I'm putting this pie in the oven now, and you be sure to bake it when you get back. Take it out after forty-five minutes." Jetta Mae took off her apron and tucked it in her bag.

Latrella and I walked right out the front door to get in the car. Joseph came running out behind us.

"I'm going too," he said as he slipped in beside me. "Latrella, do you have a brother?"

"Yes, but he's older than I am. He's fifteen." She hugged her book again.

"Aw shucks. If he were my age, I could play with him."

"Jetta Mae," Mom said, "you sit up front since the girls and Joseph are in the back."

Mom drove down the street, and when we came to the end of the sidewalk, Latrella leaned forward and tapped Mom on the shoulder.

"If you let me out here, I can run right through the woods and be home lickety-split."

"Sit tight. I am taking you right to your grandmother's front door," Mom said. She drove on down the street and turned onto

Lynch and then onto Latrella's street. Latrella pointed to a small clapboard house with blue shutters on the front window. A window box with mums in it brightened the front porch. When Mom stopped, Latrella jumped out of the car and ran up the steps.

"Bye, and thanks for the ride," she yelled, then she opened the screen door and disappeared.

Mom turned around where the charred remains of the store marked the ground. Then she took Jetta Mae home.

"Thanks, Mrs. Scuffer, and Happy Thanksgiving." Jetta Mae squeezed my hand as she left to go into her house.

I climbed into the front seat, which was still warm from Jetta Mae sitting there. "Thanks for taking them home," I said.

"It was the quickest thing to do." Mom ran her fingers through her hair.

"I gave Latrella our phone number. I hope that's okay. At least we can talk on the phone."

"If it's alright with her parents, it's alright with me."

After we got out of the car at home, I put my arm around Mom's waist, and she put hers around my shoulder. My heart beat like a metronome on fast speed as we walked together up the steps. The sun had started to set and turned the sky a pretty pink. I tucked this moment away in my memory and wished for more times just like this one.

CHAPTER 33

DELICIOUS SCENTS of roasted turkey and biscuits filled the house as Mom prepared for Thanksgiving. Jetta Mae had made it easy for Mom with all the things she fixed ahead of time. She had even already made the biscuits and placed them on a cookie sheet. All Mom had to do was take everything out of the refrigerator and stick it in the oven.

"Gertrude, please set the table," Mom said. "Aunt Liz, Sarah Jane, and Frank will be here in a few minutes. Get my china out of the buffet."

As I started to place the cloth napkins and silver at each place, the front door opened and Frank ran in, followed by Aunt Liz and Sarah Jane. It was like old times.

"We're here," Frank shouted. "Happy Thanksgiving."

Joseph ran into the living room to greet him, then they ran right through the kitchen into the backyard. Sarah Jane gave me a hug.

"Can I help you?" she asked, and I nodded. She put out the plates and glasses while I placed the napkins and silverware on the lace tablecloth. Mom always had a fancy table for Thanksgiving and Christmas.

When we all sat down, our eyes lit up at the sight of the golden-brown turkey stuffed with dressing, the sweet potatoes with

THE END OF THE SIDEWALK

yummy marshmallows on top, the peas, the gravy, and the biscuits. Dad started with the blessing and then it was our tradition for each person at the table to give thanks for one thing or one person. "I'm thankful for my family—all of you," Dad said as he smiled at us.

"My friends," Joseph said. He nudged Frank who sat beside him.

"Baseball," Frank said. We giggled at his choice.

"Trudy," Sarah Jane said when it was her turn.

"Sarah Jane," I said. "She's the best."

"For Bill's service to our country," Aunt Liz said. "Today is the anniversary of him being listed as missing in action." Aunt Liz dabbed at her eyes, and I grabbed Sarah Jane's hand under the table.

"For our families, and may God bless America. Amen," Mom said.

After supper, we filled up on pecan pie and my favorite, butterscotch pie. Sarah Jane and I got extra-big slices of butterscotch pie, and the meringue sparkled on top of the delicious custard. Our tummies were so full we could hardly move. We helped Mom and Aunt Liz with the dishes until they said it was okay to go outside, then we headed for Miss Magnolia. It felt like we were back to the way things used to be.

"Latrella's grandmother is moving in with Latrella's parents," I said, "and I told Dad about us meeting. He said we couldn't do it anymore."

"I told you shouldn't do it."

"You were right," I said. "Mom said we could talk on the phone though."

"Don't mention her around my mom," she replied. "She thinks it's too soon for us to be mingling with Colored children."

"I won't say anything, but I don't see anything wrong with it, especially since Latrella's kin to Jetta Mae. I'm glad to have her as a friend. You'd like her. She's spunky." I pulled a cone off the tree and started pulling the red seeds out.

"I'm not going to say anything about Latrella, Girl Scout honor. It's no one's business anyway."

The sky darkened, then we heard Dad's shrill whistle calling us inside.

"Let's see if your mom will let you spend the night," I said as we ran up the back steps. When we got into the kitchen, I said, "Aunt Liz, can Sarah Jane spend the night? Please?"

"I don't think so. She can come over in the morning though," she answered.

"Oh, please," I begged. "She hasn't spent the night in forever."

"Let her stay," Mom said as she put the last glass away in the cabinet. "They don't have school tomorrow."

"She has a project she needs to work on," Aunt Liz said. Sarah Jane looked at her mom with pleading eyes but didn't say a word.

"Sarah Jane has all weekend to work on the project," Mom said. "Let her stay."

"If you let her stay," I said and put my arm around Sarah Jane's waist, "I'll come over and help her with her project tomorrow."

"I guess it'll be alright," she said. I could see Aunt Liz's hesitation, but I gave her a hug after she agreed.

"Can Frank stay too?" Joseph jumped up and down.

"No, maybe you can spend tomorrow night together," Aunt Liz said. She gathered up her things. "You girls ride over to the house with me and get Sarah Jane's clothes."

We ran to get in the car. After we got her stuff, Aunt Liz watched us across the dimly lit street. The full moon lit the way for us as we raced back to my house.

When we snuggled down under the covers, I wiggled my toes. She'd settled in on the top bunk.

"I've got a secret to tell you," I whispered, "but you gotta promise you won't tell."

"What?" she asked. She had the quilt pulled up to her chin with only her head sticking out.

I got out of bed to stand on it so I could see her. "I think Wes may like me, and I think I like him too." I giggled as I revealed the idea that had been stirring in my head ever since the tennis match.

"Good choice," she said. "When did all this start?"

"Well, you remember he's in my science lab. One day we went to the library together, and then he came to the tennis match. Of course, he may have been coming to see Susan play because they've been friends since third grade." I got down on my bed and lay back on the pillow.

"Now that I think about it," Sarah Jane said, "I saw him cheering for you at the game. I think he does like you."

Mom stuck her head in the door. "Goodnight, girls. Sweet dreams to you."

"Goodnight," we said in unison. We talked for a few more minutes.

"What do you want for Christmas?" I asked. There wasn't an answer. I repeated myself but still got no answer. I wondered how she could fall asleep so fast.

I must have fallen asleep at some point because the next thing I heard was Skipper barking. I got up and shook Sarah Jane.

"Wake up. Skipper's barking at something."

"Probably a possum," she said. We crept down the hall. I looked out the front windows. "Something's on fire!" I yelled.

Sarah Jane screamed and grabbed my shoulder in a viselike grip.

"Mom, Dad, Joseph!" I yelled. "Wake up! Our house is on fire!"

Dad came running down the hall and pushed ahead of us to look out the window. "What now?" he yelled. He was already at the front door when Mom ran into the room, pulling her robe around her.

"Trudy, go get your brother up right now," she ordered.

I ran to Joseph's room and shook him hard. I couldn't believe he'd slept through our screaming. "Get up, something's burning. Hurry."

Running back to the living room, Sarah Jane was huddled on the couch with her knees pulled up to her chin.

"Lord in Heaven," Mom said. Dad had opened the door. Mom grabbed his arm. "Don't go out there. Call the police."

"It's a cross burning," Dad said. "Some fool put a burning cross in our yard." Dad wrenched his arm from Mom. "You take care of the children. Call the police. I'm going to put it out before the fire spreads."

He started out the door but then stopped and ran to the back. He brought the hose through the house.

Mom ran to the phone and dialed. "Please send someone right away to 955 Pecan Boulevard," she said. "A cross is burning in our yard."

Then she came to sit with us. Sarah Jane sobbed. I cried too. Joseph stared at the blazing cross through the front windows. I saw the terror in Sarah Jane's eyes. We held each other tightly.

THE END OF THE SIDEWALK

"Warren, the police are on the way," Mom hollered. "Please come back inside."

Joseph started crying. "Don't let anyone hurt my daddy."

Mom put her arm around him. I could see her hand shaking.

Out of the dining room window, we saw the lights in the house next door come on. I heard the water running. Dad must have hooked up the hose. Mom went over to the front door, looking outside. I wanted to see what was happening too.

"I want to call my mom," Sarah Jane said. Mom sat down and pulled Sarah Jane to her.

"Don't cry. I know you're upset. I am, too, but we're safe. The police will be here soon. It's the Ku Klux Klan that do these cross burnings to show their disapproval of anyone supporting the Negroes. They should be arrested for this. It's a hate sign. They dress in white costumes so no one will be able to recognize them. They have done terrible things in the past to the Negroes."

We heard sirens in the distance getting louder as they came closer. Out of the window, we could see Dad squirting the water from the hose on the burning cross. Hisses filled the air like a giant snake warning us to not come close. Smoke rose in the sky. Soon a charred black cross stood smoldering. A spark glowed here and there, and small trails of smoke were still drifting from the top. Like when the store had burned, it smelled like our campfires at Girl Scout Camp.

Joseph ran to the front door. Mom stepped beside him and held his arm.

"Don't go out there," she said.

"Now who called the fire department?" Dad yelled. A fire truck with lights flashing and the siren winding down stopped right by the red fire hydrant in front of our house. Two firemen, dressed in their fire gear, jumped off the truck and ran toward Dad.

Mom moved on to the front porch with Joseph, so Sarah Jane and I joined them. Lights in more houses on our street had come on, and some of our neighbors stood on their front porches. We could see their silhouettes in the night shadows.

"Sir, what happened?" one fireman asked.

"Are you blind?" Dad shouted angrily. "Some fool burned a cross in our yard. I've already put it out. You can leave now."

More sirens and flashing lights at the end of the street filled the night as two police cars arrived. The policemen jumped out and approached Dad and the firemen.

"We were called about a disturbance here," one policeman said.

"You're right. I'm quite disturbed that the Ku Klux Klan burns a cross in my yard and thinks they're above the law. I'd like for you to find out who did this and arrest them. They could have caught my house on fire. I'm a law-abiding citizen. I don't want my family subjected to such senseless, hateful actions." Dad shook his head. He went over and kicked the charred cross, knocking it on the ground.

"Sir, we'll get that for you. "We'll discard it," one fireman said and stepped toward Dad.

"No, Warren, stop them," Mom said. "Have them put the cross in the backyard. I need to think about what to do."

The firemen wrapped the charred boards of the cross with water-soaked cloths, then carried it to the back gate. Joseph sat on the steps. Lights started going off in the houses as the neighbors went back inside.

"Sorry for the disturbance, ma'am," a policeman said as he tipped his hat to us. "You best get those children back in bed. We'll patrol the neighborhood."

Mom said to us, "Come on, let's go inside. We all need to get some sleep." Mom opened the front door and motioned to us to follow her.

"Sir, I'd advise your wife to consider her family," the policeman said as Dad started up the steps.

"With all due respect, sir," Dad said, "we'll take care of our own. You just need to do your job of protecting all the people of Jackson. Now if you don't mind, we're going to bed."

We scrambled through the door as Mom followed with Dad right behind her, closing the door a little harder than usual. Sarah Jane started crying again as we went down the hall to my room.

CHAPTER 34

ONCE IN MY ROOM, Sarah Jane fell on my bed, burying her head in the pillow. I sat down beside her, not knowing what to say.

"Please don't cry." I put my hand on her shoulder. "Talk to me. Tell me what I can do."

"I want to go home. I'm scared."

She was sobbing, so I got her a tissue, and she wiped her nose as she sat up on the bed.

"I'm scared, too," I said, "but we can't call your mom now. It would frighten her out of her mind. She'd come over and get upset with Mom all over again. I want us to be able to be best friends and play together. I don't like all these mean people thinking Mom is wrong. She's trying to be helpful." Sarah Jane and I sat facing each other on my bed with our legs crossed.

"I know your mom's doing a good thing," she said, "but I don't like all this scary stuff that's happening."

"I don't like it either. I keep hoping these scary things will stop happening. I want everybody to be happy."

"Why do you think they're always picking on Colored people?" Sarah Jane sighed and lay back on the pillow.

"A lot of white people think that Negroes aren't equal to us just because of the color of their skin and because of history when they were slaves. Mom's trying to change that."

"I wonder how long it'll take. I guess we better get some sleep. I'm tired. We can talk more tomorrow," she said, yawning as she climbed up to her bed. She got back under the covers, turned over, and closed her eyes.

I tried to go to sleep, but I tossed and turned. Every little noise made me jump. I heard Sarah Jane squirming around in the bed too. At least she'd stopped crying.

"Come with me," I whispered to her. "I know something that'll help us sleep."

We tiptoed down the hall and went into the kitchen. I closed the door, turned on the light, got two glasses, and filled them with milk. Then I got the butter cookies from the Jeweled Tea salesman out of the pantry. Sarah Jane smiled. She and I loved dunking the cookies in our milk and then letting them melt in our mouth. The Jeweled Tea salesman came around once a month and sold things like dishes and cookies and all sorts of stuff.

We sat at the table, slipping our cookies down in the milk and then savoring the tasty melt in our mouths. Joseph appeared in the kitchen and yawned.

"I want some milk and cookies too," he said. I got a glass of milk for him and gave him a couple of the cookies.

"This was a good idea," Sarah Jane said as she yawned. She drank her milk down to the last drop. I finished mine and put away the cookies.

"I have another idea," I said. "I'll bring Skipper in and let him sleep with us. That way, we'll feel safer."

"Can I sleep with you too?" Joseph said. "I'll bring my pillow and spread and sleep on the floor. Please?"

"Yes," I replied. I didn't want Joseph to be scared.

"Here, Skipper," I called and whistled softly after I'd opened the back door. He came out from under the porch and trotted up the steps, wagging his tail. "Shhh. Be quiet, Skip. I want you to come and sleep with us. We're scared. You can protect us." I held on to his collar as we tiptoed back down the hall and into my room. Sure enough, we all dropped right off to sleep.

The next day, newspaper reporters called Mom and wanted an interview. Dad said no because he didn't want her picture all over the paper. He was worried about his job. But by Sunday, the front page of the paper featured an article about the cross burning. After Dad read it, he shook his head. We were all sitting in the living room, dressed for church.

"I know I'll have some repercussions at work," Dad fumed.

"Surely they won't fire you," Mom said. "You're too valuable to them."

"I don't know. The White Citizens Council may put pressure on the company, since Mr. Ross is on their board. Publicity is one thing I wanted to avoid, and a cross burning isn't an everyday happening. Why on earth do you want to keep that cross anyway? It's charred and a grim reminder of the hateful attitude of the Klan."

"I can't explain it. I'm angry and upset, but I need to think about it some more. Come on, let's go to church."

As soon as we arrived at church, a lady came running over to Mom, saying, "June, are you okay? I heard about the terrible thing that happened. I'm so sorry."

"We're all fine," Mom replied.

When we walked into church, Mom and Dad led us right up to the front pew. After the service, Sarah Jane joined me outside.

THE END OF THE SIDEWALK

"Mom's horrified about what happened, but she's not mad at your mom like I thought she would be."

Before I could reply to her, another lady came up to Mom and said, "I hope this incident convinces you to abandon the commission."

"No, it doesn't," Mom stated as she walked on down the sidewalk.

I grabbed Mom's hand and whispered, "Why didn't you tell her to mind her own business?"

"It's not the time or place to talk about it. I'm still upset over what happened, and I don't want to say something that I would regret later. I must pray about what I'm going to do."

"We're not going to move, are we?" I feared having to start over somewhere new.

"No, we aren't, but I may have to make some changes. I don't want these acts of hate to put us in any danger."

As we walked to the car, I told Mom how I felt. "I'm scared every night when I go to bed and so is Joseph. He's been sleeping in my room almost every night."

"I'm sorry you're scared. I can't guarantee we won't have more night interruptions, but your safety is important to us. Your dad and I will do all we can to make you feel safe in our home. You can come to us anytime you're scared or upset. I'll talk to Joseph about it too."

"Thanks, Mom. I know what you're doing is important, but sometimes I wish it wasn't so hard."

"I wish that, too, but you're growing up, and you'll face many challenges, not just here in Jackson, but in your own life. I'm proud of you for caring and for being honest." She squeezed my hand.

Joseph and Dad were already in the car, so we hurried to join them. When we drove by the pasture, I saw Whisper standing by the fence.

"Hey, Dad, maybe I could keep a horse there. Those people have a horse and plenty of grass. It would be convenient. I could walk there and help take care of their horse and mine."

"I think you have all the details worked out except for the money. Besides, I don't even know who those people are that live there."

"Maybe I could walk up there and talk to them."

"No, I don't think that's a good idea. It's a long walk up their drive, and you can't trespass on someone's property."

"Okay," I said. I'd expected that to be his answer, but it was worth a try. Someday, somehow, I would have a horse.

CHAPTER 35

AFTER THE Thanksgiving holiday break, I wasn't scared about going to school even though I felt sure that somebody would have something to say about the cross burning. Excited to see Susan and Wes, I hoped they would be understanding if they knew about it.

"Do you want me to walk with you into school this morning?" Mom asked as if she anticipated that people might say ugly things like the lady at church had said to her.

"No, Mom. I'll be fine."

I made it to the first-period classroom without encountering any comments from anyone in the hall. Mrs. Bailey started my day off right by reading to us the poem "Trees" by Joyce Kilmer. I thought of Miss Magnolia as she read each verse. It surprised me to learn that Joyce Kilmer was a man. He had a girl's name as his first name, like I had a boy's name, Randolph, as a middle name. I recited the first line of the poem in my mind as I left class, I decided to ask the teacher for a copy of the poem, so I could memorize the rest of the poem and to recite it to Miss Magnolia and to Latrella. I knew she would like it as much as I did.

Susan met me in the hall. "Are you okay? I bet you were freaked out with all that happened. Dennis went on a rant about how we would be taken over by the Negroes—except he used a bad word for them—if we didn't keep them in their place. He said your mom got what she deserved. But don't worry. He can't stop us from being friends."

Once we were seated in class, Wes walked by my desk and dropped a paper folded into a triangle on my desk. He smiled at me as he sat down at his desk. I opened the note and read it.

Trudy,

I saw in the newspaper what happened with the burning cross in your yard. I'm sorry. I know that must have been scary. Hey, can I have your phone number?

Wes

My heart did double palpitations. I folded the note back up and stuck it in my notebook. I'd never had a boy ask for my phone number. I glanced over at Wes and nodded with a grin. I wrote my number on a piece of paper, folded it into a triangle, and handed it to him as we left science lab. Our fingers touched for a brief second. I felt as light as a feather floating down the hallway.

That afternoon, right before I went to chorus, I went by my locker to leave my books. Wes came up behind me. "Can I walk you to class?"

"Sure," I was flabbergasted but happy about strolling to class with Wes.

"Do you think you'd like to go caroling with my church youth group on the 18th? It's a lot of fun," he said.

"I'd like to, but I'll have to ask my parents. I think they'll say yes, though." I couldn't believe it. He was asking me out. And I had worried all this time about boys not liking me.

When we got to the door, one of those sassy girls came up to me. She bumped my arm and said, "I read in the paper about the commotion at your house the other night. Serves your mom right."

"Leave her alone," Wes said, adjusting his glasses.

"Who's talking to you?" she said.

"It's okay," I said to Wes, then I looked at her square in the eye. "It won't stop my mom, and I'm proud of her."

"See ya," said Wes as he touched my shoulder, then he frowned at the girl and headed on to his class.

She stared at me, mumbled something, and turned to go to her seat. I hadn't let her send me into silent mode. I was a little flustered, but I felt good about standing up for Mom.

"All right, students," Mr. Richardson said. "Let's get started. Let's go over 'Let There Be Peace on Earth.' We'll be singing it at our Christmas concert." He picked up his baton and waved it at us to begin.

As we sang the words, I thought of my encounter with that girl. Could we ever walk in perfect harmony as the song said? After class, I left with Susan.

CHAPTER 36

AFTER SCHOOL I rounded the corner of my street. My neighbor up the street, Mr. Allen, was covering his yard with a soft white cloth that looked like snow, and I knew he was setting up his Christmas decoration. Several boxes sat on the ground beside him. Familiar models of buildings lined the driveway.

"Hi, Mr. Allen," I said. "Are you already putting out your little village? It's my favorite Christmas decoration."

"Well, young lady, it'll take two or three days to get it all hooked up and ready. People have already started asking when they can come to see it."

I peered into the church, a replica of the cathedral downtown. It even had stained glass windows. In the front, there was a miniature manger scene.

"I'll be checking each day," I said. "I know you'll have lots of people stopping by."

"I'm glad it pleases you. I love making the houses and setting them up. Mrs. Allen stays busy making all the miniature figures." He got out a wooden sleigh and two plastic horses.

Mr. Allen even had music piped into the little church so that carols played throughout the holiday season. Cars always lined our street as people from all over Jackson came to see the village. I could hardly wait until he assembled it all.

THE END OF THE SIDEWALK

When I got home, I rushed in to see Jetta Mae before she left. I wanted to find out her reaction to the cross burning. I was still rattled by it, but I was glad Mom and I had talked about it. She'd come in my room last night, and Joseph was there, so we'd sung some camp songs for him. Then she'd kissed us both and said, "Come and get me if you get scared."

I found Jetta Mae in the backyard taking some clothes off the line.

"Hey, do you need some help?" I ran out and grabbed one end of a sheet as she unpinned it and stuck the clothespins in her apron pocket.

"You're here at the right time and can help me fold these." The cool breeze sent leaves flying all around us.

"Did you see the cross?" I asked. "Did Mom tell you all about it?"

"She did. It's sad. I don't know what our world is coming to."

As we worked with the sheets, I hummed "Let There Be Peace on Earth."

"Now that is one beautiful tune. Sing the words for me." She took the basket of sheets and headed up the steps with me singing behind her.

After I finished, I said, "Jetta Mae, do you think one day we could ride the bus and sit together?"

"Girl, you're still talking about that bus. Maybe we could do that one day. I'll sure think about it. Might as well try out the new law sometime."

"Oh, I was hoping you'd agree. One day next week, okay?"

Later, I went back out and sat cross-legged in front of the charred cross. Putting my elbows on my knees, I propped my chin in my hands. What could we do with the cross? How could we show people we weren't scared of them? I wanted to help Mom think of something. Maybe if I went to sit in Miss Magnolia, I could put on my thinking cap and figure out a plan.

As I climbed up in her branches, I thought of the poem Mrs. Bailey had read. I looked to see if Miss Magnolia had a robin nest, like the poem said. I didn't see any, but the leaves were thick. I started singing "Let There Be Peace on Earth" again.

"That's it," I shouted. "We'll make a sign that says Peace on Earth and put the cross in front of it," I said to Miss Magnolia since no one else was around. "And we'll decorate the cross so it doesn't look ugly. It'll be our Christmas decoration." I thought about the tiny manger scene in front of the church in Mr. Allen's yard. "We can add a nativity scene too."

I scrambled out of the tree and rushed to tell Jetta Mae. When I opened the back door, I heard her calling me.

"Here I am," I said as I peeked my head around the door.

"Phone call for you." She handed me the phone. I took it, pressed it to my ear, and said hello.

"Hi, it's Wes."

My fingers started to tremble around the phone. "I was in my backyard." Once we started talking, I calmed down. Before I knew it, I said, "Let me read you a poem I heard in English today. I liked it so much that I want to memorize it. Just a minute." I put the phone down, ran to get my things, then came back and picked the phone up again. "It's a poem titled 'Trees' by Joyce Kilmer, and it goes,

I think that I shall never see
A poem lovely as a tree.
A tree whose hungry mouth is prest
Against the earth's sweet flowing breast;
A tree that looks at God all day,
And lifts her leafy arms to pray;
A tree that may in Summer wear
A nest of robins in her hair;
Upon whose bosom snow has lain;
Who intimately lives with rain.
Poems are made by fools like me,
But only God can make a tree."

After I paused to take a breath, I said, "Did you know Joyce Kilmer is a man? I have a tree in my backyard I call Miss Magnolia. I like to climb up it and spend time there. Do you think that's silly?"

"No, I didn't know Joyce Kilmer was a man," Wes said. "I surely don't know any guys named Joyce. And no, I don't think you're silly. I like trees too. I have an oak tree in my yard that I like to climb. I like that poem too. My mom likes poems. I'll have to see if she knows that one. Did you ask about the caroling? My mom said she would talk to your mom."

"I haven't asked her yet. Just a minute. I'll get her and you get your mom." I covered the phone and called for Mom. She came to the phone, and I said, "It's my friend Wes from school on the phone. He's invited me to go caroling with his church youth group in a couple of weeks. His mom wants to talk to you."

I handed her the phone. She talked for a few minutes, and

I heard her say, "That'll be fine. It's good to connect with you again." She smiled as she handed the phone back to me, and I put it to my ear.

"Your mom says you can go," Wes said. "That's great." We talked a few minutes more until I saw Jetta Mae get ready to leave. "Well, I'll see you tomorrow, Wes. Thanks for calling."

After I hung up, I ran out to the car to ride with Mom as she took Jetta Mae home. Jetta Mae had moved to the street next to her sister. It was a long way from our house, and I would miss walking her to the end of the sidewalk. It was a bigger house with a screened porch on the front. This was another change for me, but I was happy for Jetta Mae.

When I got home, the phone was ringing. "Hello, Scuffer residence," I said.

"Is this three-five-three-dash-six-seven-five-six?" I laughed as Latrella sang my number.

"Yes, it is, can I help you?" She laughed and then she got serious.

"Sorry about the cross burning. Dad saw it in the paper. I'm certain it was really scary. The Klan is crazy with hate. They should find something better to do than harass people."

"It was awful. Sarah Jane had spent the night, and we were both screaming and crying. Mom tried to calm us down. She was scared too. I saw her hand shaking. Joseph was scared for my dad, but he liked seeing the fire truck. Dad was so angry. He put the fire out before the police and firemen got here. Dad said this kind of hate has been going on for a long time."

Latrella said, "I'll say. All my life and more. They make me sick to my stomach."

"I have some good news. Wes asked me to go caroling with him and his church group, and Mom said I could."

"So, you're in love," she said.

"No way, but I'm excited about going caroling. Wes is a neat guy. Anyway, I'll keep you posted on what happens. Thanks for calling. Bye."

When I got off the phone, I started humming "Let There Be Peace on Earth." I couldn't get that song out of my head.

"Sing that song for me," Mom said. I started singing, and she smiled the whole time until I finished.

"Mom, the song gave me an idea about how we might use the cross." I told her about the banner, the cross, and the nativity scene. "Mr. Allen's display gave me the idea of the nativity scene. He has that little one in front of the church in his yard."

"I like that. I'll get your dad to set up a spotlight that shines on the display at night. It'll be the perfect Christmas decoration. I knew I could count on you to think of something."

I had a warm feeling from the tip-top of my head to the end of my little toe. Mom liked my plan and wanted to do it. "I love you, Mom."

"I love you too. Let's go shopping tomorrow for the nativity scene."

The next day Mom picked me up after school to go shopping.

At the store, we found figures of Joseph, Mary, and baby Jesus that would light up at night. We got plenty of garland for the cross. Mom bought a poster board and gold glitter. She also purchased black material for the banner.

When we got home, we started cutting out the letters to put on the banner. Joseph came in to watch us.

"Let me help," he said.

Mom let him put glitter on the letters as she and I cut them out. We pinned the gold glittery letters to the black material and would wrap the cross with the garland, leaving some of the charred parts visible. Mom usually waited until the week before Christmas to put up any decorations, but this year, she wanted to get the message out as soon as possible.

When Dad came home and saw us busy at the dining room table, he asked, "What on earth are you doing?"

Mom explained our plan and Dad smiled. "Why, Gertrude, aren't you smart?" I didn't feel smart, but I liked his compliment.

"I got the idea from this song we sing at school about peace."

After supper, we went out in the front yard to set things up. Dad hammered the cross into the ground right beside the hole made by the dynamite, and Mom put the garland on it. Joseph and I stretched the banner while Dad stuck the poles in the ground to hold it up. The gold letters sparkled like they were covered with a million little stars. Mom placed Joseph, Mary, and baby Jesus in front of the cross. Then Dad hooked up the spotlight.

When it got dark, Dad turned it on. The light cast a huge shadow of a cross on our house. The message glittered as the light shone on it.

"Can I call Sarah Jane to come and see it?" I asked. "Yes," Mom said.

I ran inside and called Sarah Jane. "Ask your mom to bring you over right now to see something very important. It won't take long, but you need to see it. Please."

I went back outside, and we stood on the sidewalk looking at the display. Dad had turned the spotlight off, then Sarah Jane,

Frank, and Aunt Liz arrived.

"What's going on?" Frank yelled as he jumped out of the car and joined us on the sidewalk.

Dad turned on the light again. I put my one arm around Sarah Jane's shoulder. Mom and Aunt Liz joined us. Dad put his arms around Joseph and Frank. We all stood there in silence for a minute.

"The cross of hate is now a cross of love," Mom whispered as the faint strains of "Silent Night" drifted through the air from Mr. Allen's church up the street. We sang along to the melody. Mom had her eyes closed and a soft smile on her face.

I knew Mom had a big heart and loved everyone. I wanted to be like her. I closed my eyes and tried to imagine myself as a mom one day. I knew I would share this moment with my children as a special memory. Maybe by then things would be different than they were now, and everyone would get along better.

Dad said, "I think we could all use some hot chocolate and cookies."

And he jolted me back to the present.

"Yummy. Let's go right now," Joseph said as he ran up the steps and held the door. We all walked into the house, Sarah Jane and me arm in arm followed by Mom, Aunt Liz, Frank, Joseph, and Dad. Faint sounds of Christmas music floated through the air.

CHAPTER 37

THE NEXT DAY I marched up to the fence on Claiborne with a carrot in one pocket and an apple in the other. I whistled and saw Whisper trotting toward me. Ah, if he were only my horse for real. I sat on the top rail. He nudged my pocket with his nose.

"Watch out or you'll knock me over," I said. I reached in my pocket for the carrot first. He stood there munching while I stroked his mane. Then he nudged me again.

"Are you greedy? I do have a bonus for you since Christmas is almost here and I promised." I took out the apple and gave it to him. Some fell on the ground as he crunched it. He leaned down and cleaned up every bit.

"That's all for now, sweet boy. See you later." He moved his head up and down as if he was nodding to me. I climbed down, took one last look as he moved away from the fence, and ran home.

A cold breeze blew through the bare trees. I wished it would snow, but that was unlikely. It had last snowed in Jackson when I was six years old. It was an ice storm, and Dad had made a sled and pulled us up and down the street. I'd held Joseph in front of me. He was only two, so he didn't remember, but I did. I loved this time of year. Tonight was the caroling event with Wes's church.

That evening when I opened the door and saw him standing there, a weakness came over me, and I thought I might faint. I

THE END OF THE SIDEWALK

swallowed hard, took three deep breaths, and jiggled my knees back and forth. My strength returned, and I managed to say hi. Mom came to the door with my gloves in her hand.

"You might need these," she said. "Have a good time. Good to see you, Wes."

His mother took us to the church, and we joined the group. He knew them all, but I recognized only a few people from school. He introduced me to several of his friends. We went around the neighborhood right by his church singing one carol in front of each house. At one house, the whole family came out on their porch. When we finished our carol and said Merry Christmas, a little boy about five yelled to please sing "Rudolph the Red-Nosed Reindeer." We all laughed and sang it for him. He joined in with us and clapped when we finished.

As we started back to the church, Wes took my hand. We both had on gloves, but it still felt special. They served us cocoa and cookies before leaving. On the way home, we told his mom about the kid who requested Rudolph. When we got to my house, he walked me to the door.

"That was fun, and I had a great time," I said.

He gave me a hug and said, "Me too. Merry Christmas, Trudy."

In the house, our tree stood in the corner of the living room. The aroma of cedar filled the air. Bright lights and tinsel sparkled on the tree. I wanted to dance down the hall.

"Did you have a good time?" Dad asked.

"Oh, yes. It was wonderful." Could Dad tell my face was flushed and that I couldn't stop smiling?

On Christmas Eve, we went to bed early, but Mom woke us up at 10:30 for the Midnight Service at our church. We traipsed through the living room, our empty stockings hanging on the mantel.

The church was decorated with greenery and lit with candles, which made it feel magical. It was my favorite service, singing Christmas carols and being with my family. Sarah Jane and I had on the same red taffeta dresses, as if we were twins. We all sat together and filled up one pew. I tried hard to listen to the sermon, but I started getting sleepy. I must have dozed off for a few seconds because when the organist started playing, I jumped. Sarah Jane snickered and poked me. The service ended with a rousing chorus of "O Come, All Ye Faithful."

On the way home, I looked up into the night sky. We used to look for Santa and his reindeer, but this year, Joseph didn't even mention it. It used to be that if we saw a red airplane light, we would think it was Rudolph. I wasn't sure if Joseph would do it, but I decided to give it a try.

"Let's look for Santa. Maybe he has Rudolph this year."

Joseph peered out his window, and I looked out mine. I'd like to think he had at least one more year of believing.

The next day, we didn't open any gifts until Aunt Liz, Sarah Jane, and Frank arrived. Often, they came and stayed the whole day. Would this year be any different? Joseph was itching to start. When they arrived late in the morning, Joseph whooped it up like he was at a rodeo.

We all opened our presents. I got a real cowboy hat and some brand-new cowboy boots. I decided right then and there that I'd wear my cowboy boots to school. I didn't care what anyone said.

We took our full stockings down. We always got an orange and apple along with candy and pencils and other little things.

THE END OF THE SIDEWALK

This year, a white envelope was in mine. I opened it, and when I read what it said, I started crying tears of joy. It wasn't a promise of a horse, but it was a certificate for ten riding lessons at the stable where I rode with Katie. I jumped up and hugged Mom and Dad.

Sarah Jane gave me a book on horses, so I was all set. I'd given Sarah a heart necklace with my name on one side and hers on the other. She wanted me to help her fasten it on her neck, then she and I hugged. Mom and Aunt Liz sat chatting and smiling at each other. Joseph and Frank played a game of checkers. Dad read a new book he'd gotten.

We'd been through some frightening experiences, but none like the Negroes had been living through for years. I'd learned a lot from Jetta Mae, from Latrella, from the Freedom Riders, and from Mom and Dad about the hatred the Negroes had endured, and I knew why they were standing up for their rights. If Mom hadn't been involved in the commission, I wouldn't have known these things. And I wouldn't have understood that we didn't all have to think the same way to love each other.

I looked around at all my family and saw happy faces. I wanted to grab this moment and make it last. Though things weren't perfect, they were better. Together we would face the good times and the hard times as a family.

PHOTOS

My dog, Skipper

My parents, Jane and Wallie

THE END OF THE SIDEWALK

My cousin Jane with me

The dining room table

Nancy Schutt McCorkle

Villa Ree, our housekeeper

My house, showing the sidewalk and fire hydrant

THE END OF THE SIDEWALK

My cousins, Jane and Freddy, with me and my brother John

Me at the end of the sidewalk

ACKNOWLEDGMENTS

INITIALLY, I want to express my heartfelt gratitude to the late Pat Fox and the Coastal Georgia Writing Project for starting me on my writing journey. Thanks to Debbie Rotkow, my first writing group critique partner, for always supporting and encouraging me, and to Nina Delk, my teaching cohort, with whom I attended many writing conferences.

In 2008, my cousin and I attended the Wildacres Writing Workshop in the Blue Ridge Mountains of North Carolina, where my novel was born. We returned for two more summers, and I was fortunate to have Abigail Dewitt and Carrie Brown as my instructors. Along with other writers, I learned about the writing process and developing my story. Thanks to Jane Monachelli, my cousin and heart sister, for her constant presence from the beginning and for seeing me through the ups and downs of my writing journey.

My thanks go to Kristen Wolden Nitz with the Institute of Children's Literature, who guided me in writing the novel.

In 2012, I moved to Asheville, North Carolina, and participated in the Great Smokies Writing Program under the excellent instruction of Joy Neaves. Thanks to her for introducing me to the storyboard.

Thanks to Caroline Starr Rose for her edit of my manuscript and her encouraging word.

In 2014, I attended the Atlanta Writing Workshop and pitched my book to Janell Agyeman. Although she did not choose to represent me, she made some excellent suggestions to improve my manuscript. In 2024, I discovered that she had her own agency, Next Steps Literary Agency. I reached out to her, and she reviewed my manuscript again and recommended The Writer's Ally to me. I am grateful that she pointed me in that direction.

I contacted Ally Machate, and her agency has guided me through the publishing process. Thanks to Michele Rubin, my editor, who advised me in major revisions to make my book the best that it could be. Her expertise and her notable experience were invaluable to me. Thanks to Emily Hitchcock and her team for the cover design and marketing assistance. Thanks to Julie for her help in preparing the manuscript.

I am grateful for SCBWI for all the resources available to writers and illustrators for children's books. All the workshops and conferences I attended through the years have been a great benefit and an enjoyable experience.

Thanks to the Storyweavers, my writing group, and specifically to Ann Trousdale, Sharon Pragle, Kristin D'Agostino, Joyce Brown, and David Weintraub for their critiques and encouragement.

Thanks to Carolyn Scott, who read many revisions and pushed me forward when I was discouraged and who will be so glad to hold a book in her hand. Thanks to my college roommate Jean Welsh, who always provided kind words and positive vibes about my book.

Thanks to my siblings, Wallie, Pat, Ella, and John, for the times we shared growing up. Thanks to my husband, Ken, for bearing with me as I spent hours at the computer. I appreciate his patience and his love. He is forever my dandy man. Thanks to my children John, Patricia, and Page, for their support and love. This is the book of my heart, and it is a dream come true.

BIBLIOGRAPHY

Arsenault, Raymond. *Freedom Riders 1961 and the Struggle for Racial Justice*. Oxford University Press, 2006.

Barber, Barbara. *By Faith: A Century of Progress, a History of the Episcopal Church of Saint Mark, Jackson, Mississippi, 1883–2003*. iUniverse, 2009.

B*ritannica*, "Martin Luther King, Jr.," last updated August 20, 2025, https://www.britannica.com/biography/martin-luther-king-jr.

Houck, Davis W. and David Dixon, eds., *Women and the Civil Rights Movement, 1954–1965*. University Press of Mississippi, 2009.

Jane Schutt, "An Interviews with Jane Schutt, February 22, 1981," interview by John Jones and John Dittmer, Mississippi Department of Archives and History, https://da.mdah.ms.gov.

Jane M. Schutt, "An Oral History with Jane M. Schutt," interview by Leesha Faulkner for the Mississippi Oral History Program of the University of Southern Mississippi, 1994, https://crdl.usg.edu.

Kilmer, Joyce. "Trees". The Poetry Foundation. August, 2025. https://www.poetryfoundation.org/poetrymagazine/poems/12477/trees.

Le Gallienne, Richard. "I Meant to do my Work Today". August, 2025. https://www.public-domain-poetry.com/richard-le-galliene/i-meant-to-do-my-work-today-23560.

Morris, Tiyi M. *Womanpower Unlimited and the Black Freedom Struggle in Mississippi*. University of Georgia Press, 2015.

BOOKS OF INTEREST FOR YOUNG READERS

The Story of Ruby Bridges by Robert Coles (Scholastic, Inc., 2004)

The Watsons Go to Birmingham—1963 by Christopher Paul Curtis (Scholastic, Inc., 1998)

My Brother Martin by Christine King Farris (Simon and Schuster, 2003)

Ruby Lee and Me by Shannon Hitchcock (Scholastic, Inc., 2016)

Night on Fire by Ronald Kidd (Albert Whitman and Company, 2015)

Yard Wars by Taylor Kitchings (Penguin Random House, 2016)

Rosa's Bus: the Ride to Civil Rights by Jo S. Kittinger (Calkins Creek, 2010)

Yankee Girl by Mary Ann Rodman (Farrar Straus Giroux, 2004)

Glory Be by Augusta Scattergood (Scholastic, Inc., 2012)

This Is the Dream by Diana Z. Shore and Jessica Alexander (Harper Collins, 2006)

ABOUT THE AUTHOR

THIS BOOK, while a work of historical fiction, includes some events which happened to my family during the 1960s. My mother was a Civil Rights activist in Jackson, Mississippi. Her involvement led me to create a fictional story of a girl growing up during this crucial period in our history. As I wrote the story, the characters took on personalities of their own. I used the names of some real people to give credit to their work and involvement. Likewise, I used the names of real places in Jackson and nearby. I wanted to capture a sense of authenticity as the story unfolded.

Trudy and I like the same things: reading, camping, and horses. I have a cousin who is also my best friend. I did have a friend with a horse. I have four siblings instead of one, as in the story. Villa Ree Brown worked for my parents, but she and Jetta Mae have different personalities. Wes, Polly, Susan, and Latrella are all fictitious friends who played an important part in my story.

In 1996, I attended a summer program for teachers with The Coastal Georgia Writing Project. The late Pat Fox, the director, suggested to me that I should write a book about my experience. She planted the seed, but it took a long time to grow into fruition. I am grateful that I was able to nurture that seed into this story.

Made in the USA
Coppell, TX
21 December 2025

66755224R00156